# THE
# BABY-SITTER

## Books III and IV

# THE
# BABY-SITTER
## Books III and IV

# R.L. STINE

**SCHOLASTIC INC.**

New York  Toronto  London  Auckland  Sydney
Mexico City  New Delhi  Hong Kong  Buenos Aires

*The Baby-sitter III*, ISBN 0-590-46099-4
Copyright © 1993 by Robert L. Stine

*The Baby-sitter IV*, ISBN 0-590-48744-2
Copyright © 1995 by Robert L. Stine

12 11 10 9 8 7 6 5 4 3 2 1          5 6 7 8 9/0

Printed in the U.S.A.          01

This edition created exclusively for Barnes & Noble, Inc.

2005 Barnes & Noble Books

ISBN 0-7607-9590-8

This edition first printing, August 2005

# Contents

# THE BABY-SITTER III

# Chapter 1

Mr. Larson smiled at Jenny Jeffers. "The two most important rules at The Doughnut Hole," he said, rubbing his chin, "are: Don't Touch and Don't Eat. No free samples."

Jenny stared back at him. "You mean, no free samples for the customers?" she asked hesitantly.

Mr. Larson chuckled, as if she had cracked a joke. He shook his pudgy head. "No free samples for *you*! If our workers started scarfing down our doughnuts, pretty soon they wouldn't fit behind the counter. Take a look. There's not much room back here."

Jenny let her eyes roam down the long yellow counter. A woman and a little boy were seated at the far end. The boy had smeared a chocolate doughnut over most of his face. The woman was frantically trying to clean him up with a napkin.

The large yellow-and-red neon sign, suspended from the ceiling, was reflected in the long window that ran the length of the restaurant. Jenny read the words *THE DOUGHNUT HOLE* backwards in the glass. Outside the window, she could see people hurrying up and down the wide corridor of the mall.

I don't really want to work in a doughnut shop this summer, Jenny thought wistfully. It's going to be really boring. And I don't like Mr. Larson. His face is so pale and doughy, just like his doughnuts.

"So do you want the job?" he asked, wiping a round coffee stain off the counter with a damp cloth.

No. No. No, Jenny thought.

"What is the pay again?" she asked.

"Four dollars an hour."

"Yes. I'll take it," Jenny said softly.

Her mother had just been laid off from her job as a legal secretary. Jenny had no choice. She had to work this summer. They really needed the money.

"When can you start?" Mr. Larson tossed the wet cloth under the counter. An elderly couple, dressed in identical navy-blue running suits, entered the restaurant and stood staring at the display of doughnuts.

"Monday, I guess," Jenny told him. "School is out. So I guess Monday."

"Be here at six-thirty sharp. We open at seven. We do a big breakfast business."

What a summer, Jenny thought unhappily. Staring at a wall of greasy doughnuts at six-thirty every morning.

"Fine," she said, forcing a smile.

Mr. Larson reached out and shook her hand. His hand felt warm and squishy, like a jelly doughnut.

Jenny pushed open the glass door and escaped into the crowded mall. As she walked past The Doughnut Hole, she glanced back through the glass in time to see Mr. Larson stuff an entire chocolate cruller into his mouth.

Jenny had to laugh. No wonder Mr. Larson was beginning to resemble a doughnut!

Still chuckling, she walked away quickly, dodging a baby stroller, nearly colliding with a boy on Rollerblades.

Jenny's thoughts were on the summer. It won't be a lot of fun, she thought. But at least I've got a job. Mom will be happy.

She sighed as she continued down the crowded mall corridor. The job, she realized, didn't pay much better than baby-sitting.

Baby-sitting.

The word still made Jenny shudder and feel cold all over.

She'd had such horrifying experiences as a baby-sitter. She knew she'd never baby-sit again.

It was nearly two years later, and she still thought about it all the time. Two years later, and she still thought about Mr. Hagen, the man who hated baby-sitters. Jenny was the baby-sitter for the Hagens. Until Mr. Hagen had tried to kill her.

But she had lived. And he had died.

Died because of her. . . .

Dr. Schindler — he was Jenny's psychiatrist — said she was doing really well.

But Jenny wasn't so sure.

Why did she still think about Mr. Hagen so much? Why did she still dream about him? About the night he tried to push her over the edge of the rock quarry and instead went hurtling to his own death? Why did every blond little boy remind her of Donny Hagen, his son?

Wasn't it time she forgot all that had happened?

"Jenny! Hey — Jenny!" A hand grabbed Jenny's shoulder.

Startled, she spun around to find her best friends Claire and Rick grinning at her. "Didn't you hear us calling you?" Claire asked.

"No. I . . . uh . . . was thinking about something," Jenny replied. "How's it going? What are you guys doing?"

"Just hanging out," Rick said, placing a hand on Claire's shoulder. He shrugged his broad shoulders and flashed Jenny his goofy grin.

Rick was a big, good-looking teddy bear of a guy, with dark eyes that always seemed to be laughing and curly black hair that he seldom brushed. He was wearing faded jeans, torn at both knees, and a red-and-black T-shirt with the words *METAL MANIACS* emblazoned across the chest.

Claire was tall and thin, an inch or two taller than Rick, with straight brown hair swept back in a ponytail and serious brown eyes. She wasn't really pretty, but would be some day. She was wearing an enormous yellow T-shirt over black leggings.

"We were too late for the movie, so we're wandering around," Claire said. "You shopping?"

"No." Jenny shook her head. "I just had a summer job interview. At The Doughnut Hole."

"Are you going to be a doughnut?" Rick joked.

Claire shoved him away. "That was really lame, you know?"

Rick laughed. "Yeah. I know."

"I got the job," Jenny said without enthusiasm.

"Hey, that's great," Claire started. Then seeing Jenny's downcast expression, she added, "Isn't it?"

"Well . . . I need a job," Jenny replied, shoving her hands into her jeans pockets. "Dr. Schindler thinks it's a good idea for me to get out of the house and do something different this summer. And, of course, with Mom being laid off, we really need the money."

"And the free doughnuts!" Rick added with a grin.

Jenny shook her head. "No free samples," she said, imitating Mr. Larson's stern voice.

"No free samples? You should quit!" Rick declared.

Claire glared at him. "Give Jenny a break." Claire didn't like to kid around. She was a serious, caring person, and seldom made jokes. Rick was an unlikely boyfriend for Claire. He was always cracking jokes, seldom serious.

Claire turned to Jenny. "You're lucky to get a job. Most places aren't hiring this summer."

"Yeah, I know," Jenny replied quietly. She tugged a strand of dark hair off her forehead. "I'm working the morning shift, so at least I'll be free at night to see Cal."

"Does Cal have a job yet?" Rick asked.

Jenny shook her head. "Not yet."

Claire glanced at the clock over the entrance to Sutton's, the largest department store at the mall. "We have time before the next show. Come on — walk around with us."

"Okay. Good," Jenny replied, smiling. "I promised Mom I'd get the car home. But I have a little time."

"I'm just going to grab a cone at Mulligan's," Rick said, starting across the aisle toward the ice cream parlor. "Can I get you anything?"

"No thanks," Claire and Jenny replied in unison.

Claire stopped to stare at the display in a shoe store window.

A bathing suit in Sutton's window caught Jenny's eye, and she moved close to admire it.

I won't be needing a bathing suit this summer, she thought wistfully. Not at The Doughnut Hole.

When she turned away from the window, she saw him.

And froze.

He was walking toward her. A large man in a yellow windbreaker.

She saw the red face. The close-cropped brown hair.

And those eyes. Those steel-gray eyes.

*Mr. Hagen.*

*It's Mr. Hagen,* Jenny realized, gaping at the approaching figure in horror.

But he's *dead.*

I know he's *dead.*

He's dead, and he's here, walking toward me.

And what was that in his hands?

Jenny pressed her back against the window glass and stared open-mouthed.

He was carrying a baby.

Mr. Hagen — dead Mr. Hagen — was carrying a baby in his arms.

And as he drew near, he raised his steel-gray eyes to Jenny's.

His expression was blank, as blank as death.

And with a quick, simple motion, he grabbed the baby's head with one hand, twisted it, and pulled it off.

# Chapter 2

Jenny didn't realize she was screaming until Claire grabbed her shoulders.

"Jenny — stop! Jenny, what *is* it?" Claire cried.

Jenny's entire body convulsed in a shudder of terror.

"Jenny, what's *wrong?*"

Mr. Hagen gaped at her, his ruddy face twisted in surprise. He still held the baby's head in one hand, its torso cradled under his other arm.

Only it wasn't Mr. Hagen.

It was another man, Jenny saw.

Another big, red-faced man. Not Mr. Hagen.

"Jenny — are you all right?" Claire demanded, holding onto Jenny's shoulders.

"What's going on?" Rick cried, pushing his way through the crowd that had gathered. He had a double-dip chocolate cone raised in one hand.

"Is she okay?" the red-faced man asked Claire, keeping his distance, his eyes studying Jenny.

"The . . . the b-baby — " Jenny stammered, pointing with a trembling hand.

Bewildered, the man held up the baby's head. "This?"

It was a doll, Jenny saw.

Not a baby. A doll.

"I'm taking it back to the toy store," the man told her. "The head comes off."

"A doll," Jenny said weakly.

"Are you okay?" Claire asked Jenny.

"Yeah. I guess." Jenny nodded. She raised her eyes to the man. "Sorry." Her legs felt shaky. The lights shimmered. The crowd around her started to blur.

She closed her eyes.

When she opened them, the man was gone. Claire and Rick stood beside her, their faces filled with concern. "I thought — " Jenny started to explain. "I saw him pull off the head, and I thought — "

"It was a very real-looking doll," Claire said softly, glancing at Rick.

Rick's ice cream was dripping down over the cone. He licked the chocolate off the back of his hand. "Should we take you home?" he asked.

"I — I've always had a wild imagination," Jenny said unsteadily. "I guess this time I . . ." Her voice trailed off.

"Let Rick and me drive you home," Claire said tenderly.

"Thanks," Jenny replied. "My car is that way." She pointed.

*When am I going to stop seeing Mr. Hagen everywhere?* she asked herself, allowing them to lead her to the parking lot. Mr. Hagen is dead. He's been dead nearly two years.

When am I going to stop thinking about him?

*When?*


Jenny stared at herself in her dressing table mirror. I should wash my hair, she thought, straightening her wavy, brown hair with one hand.

I look terrible.

Her dark eyes were red-rimmed and bloodshot. Her normally creamy skin looked rough and blotchy.

She hadn't slept much the night before. She'd had another nightmare about Donny and Mr. Hagen, which had startled her awake at two in the morning. She'd felt edgy and irritable all day.

And now, seeing how dreadful she looked wasn't cheering Jenny up at all.

"Good news!" Mrs. Jeffers' voice broke through Jenny's glum thoughts.

She turned away from the dressing table to see her mother rush into the room, an excited smile on her face.

"You got a new job?" Jenny asked, climbing to her feet.

"No." Mrs. Jeffers bit her lower lip. "It's not about me. It's about you." She plopped down on the edge of Jenny's unmade bed.

"What's the good news?" Jenny asked, walking over to the bed and staring down at her mother. Mom really should do something about all that gray hair, Jenny thought.

"You've been invited to spend the summer with your cousin Debra," Mrs. Jeffers announced. She stared at Jenny expectantly, waiting for a happy reaction.

But all Jenny could manage was a "Huh?"

"I arranged it all with your Aunt Julia. A change of scenery will do you so much good, Jenny. It's so beautiful upstate. And you and Debra have always gotten along so well."

"But, Mom — we discussed this yesterday. I have a job for the summer," Jenny protested. "And Dr. Schindler — "

"I spoke to him about it this morning," Mrs.

Jeffers interrupted. "He thinks a change of scenery will be good for you, too."

"Well, thanks to both of you for deciding my life," Jenny snapped. "Behind my back!"

"Jenny — " Mrs. Jeffers climbed to her feet and confronted her daughter face-to-face. "We all want what's best for you, dear." She sighed. "I don't want you to go away for the summer. I'll miss you. I'll be terribly lonely. But I really think it'll be good for you to be away from here."

Jenny uttered an exasperated sigh, but didn't reply. Crossing her arms over her chest, she glared harshly at her mother.

"Jenny, sit down for a while and think about it," Mrs. Jeffers urged. "You had another nightmare last night, didn't you?"

"Maybe," Jenny replied grudgingly.

"And you thought you saw Mr. Hagen two nights ago at the Walker Mall?"

"Yeah. Well. . . ." Jenny turned away from her mother. "Am I on trial here or something?" she asked shrilly.

"Of course not," her mother replied, obviously stung by the accusation. She tried to put a comforting hand on Jenny's shoulder, but Jenny pulled out of her reach.

"Mom, listen, I appreciate what you're doing, but — " Jenny stopped in midsentence, startled by the sadness she saw on her mother's face.

Mom looks so much older, so much grayer, Jenny realized, studying her mother intently. Is it because of me?

"If you stay with your cousin, you won't have to work at The Doughnut Hole," Mrs. Jeffers continued, not giving up. "I know you weren't exactly looking forward to working there all summer, Jenny."

"How do *you* know? Maybe I'm planning a *career* in doughnuts!" Jenny declared. She had started out angry, but the absurdity of this idea made her burst out laughing.

Before they realized it, Jenny and her mother were both laughing out loud and hugging each other.

"I thought you liked Debra," Mrs. Jeffers said finally, wiping tears of laughter from her eyes with her fingers.

"I do," Jenny replied. "She's a little too perfect, though. With that perfect figure. And that perfect little face. And that perfect blonde hair."

"She's very pretty," Mrs. Jeffers agreed softly.

"And she can be very competitive," Jenny added. "She always has to win, always has to get her way."

"I guess we don't know someone else who's like that," Mrs. Jeffers said pointedly, teasing Jenny.

Jenny didn't react. She suddenly remembered Cal. "Cal and I, we planned to spend a lot of time together this summer," she said, more to herself than her mother.

"I'm sure Cal will understand," Mrs. Jeffers said. "He's worried about you, too." She glanced at herself in the dressing table mirror, then turned back to Jenny. "And maybe he can come visit you upstate."

"Yeah. Maybe," Jenny replied thoughtfully.

"So you'll go?" Mrs. Jeffers asked, bending to straighten the blanket on Jenny's bed. "Shall I call Aunt Julia?"

"I guess," Jenny said, forcing a smile. "Thanks, Mom."

A pleased grin spread across her mother's face, momentarily smoothing away the wrinkles. She crossed the room and hugged Jenny happily. "I'll miss you," she whispered.

Jenny was thinking about Cal. How would he react to this news?

She never knew how Cal would react. They had been going together for several months, but in many ways, he remained a mystery to her.

For one thing, he was so quiet. It was hard

to know what he was thinking. And he had a dark side, an angry side that he tried to keep from Jenny.

But Cal had been very understanding, very caring. And when the nightmares kept coming, when Jenny had thought she was being pursued by Mr. Hagen from beyond the grave, Cal had been there for her.

Leaning over the dressing table, she brushed her dark hair. Then she pulled a long-sleeved white sweater over her T-shirt. She took a last glance at herself, fretting about how pale she looked, then headed downstairs.

"Are you going out?" her mother called from the living room.

"I'm going over to Cal's," Jenny called to her, picking up the car keys from the table in the front hallway. "I don't want to tell him over the phone."

"Don't stay too late," Mrs. Jeffers warned. She said something else, but Jenny was already out the door.

It was a cool night for June. Wind gusts shivered the fresh leaves on the trees. The sky was red-tinged and starless, threatening rain.

With a shudder, Jenny slid onto the cold car seat and pulled the car door shut. She dropped her bag onto the passenger seat and pulled the seat belt over her chest.

She started to turn the key in the ignition, then stopped.

What was that shadow sliding across the side of the garage?

Was it a man?

She held her breath, staring hard through the windshield.

Was someone there?

No. No one.

Trees bent in the gusting wind. The late tulips by the front porch bobbed and trembled.

No one there.

Just my imagination again, Jenny thought, starting to breathe. Every shadow scares me.

I think someone is hiding in every shadow.

I really *do* have to get away from here.

Feeling jittery, she backed down the driveway and drove across town to Cal's house. She parked at the curb across the street from his house and cut the lights. Then, pushing open the door, she climbed out and, leaning on the car door, took a deep breath, trying to steady herself.

She stared down the block of small, box-shaped houses.

Cal's block is so dark, she thought. The streetlights were all out. The houses were black shadows against the red-gray sky.

Turning her eyes to Cal's house, she saw

orange light in an upstairs window. Cal must be up in his room, she thought.

She had started to cross the street when she heard footsteps behind her.

Hurried footsteps.

With a silent gasp, she started to jog.

The footsteps behind her moved faster.

This wasn't a shadow, she knew.

This wasn't her imagination.

Someone was chasing her.

# Chapter 3

Jenny's sneakers slapped the dark driveway as she ran. She gasped for air. Her chest throbbed with pain.

"Hey — !" A breathless voice behind her. "Hey — !"

She heard gruff wheezing at her ankles. An animal sound.

"Hey — stop!" The breathless voice, pleading.

"Oh!" Jenny cried. The animal uttered a low grunt and darted in front of her, blocking her path.

It was a dog, she saw. A small terrier.

Jenny wheeled around to face her pursuer. "What do you want?" The words burst out of her in a shrill voice she didn't recognize.

The man stopped a few yards behind her, breathing heavily. He was middle-aged, maybe fifty or so, very overweight and balding, dressed in baggy shorts and a big sweatshirt. He held up her bag. "You dropped this."

"Oh." Jenny felt the blood rushing to her head, felt her face grow hot. "I — I'm sorry. You scared me," she said.

"I was walking Petey," the man said, pointing to the terrier who was sniffing the side of the stoop. "I saw you drop your bag when you got out of the car." He blew out a long breath. "Whew! Quite a chase!"

"I'm really sorry," Jenny told him, taking the bag from his hand. "It — it's so dark. I heard someone behind me, and — "

The man chuckled. "I guess Petey and I look like pretty desperate characters."

"No. I — I just got scared," Jenny explained. "I'm really sorry. Thanks. I mean, for the bag."

The man said good night and coaxed the dog away from the stoop. Jenny watched them disappear around the corner.

What am I going to do? she thought, ringing Cal's doorbell with a trembling hand.

*I'm turning into a total nut case!*

The porch light flashed on. The door opened. Cal's pale blue eyes went wide in surprise. "Jenny — hi!"

He pushed open the screen door to let her in. His spiky blond hair looked almost platinum in the white porch light. The gold stud in his ear caught the light and gleamed for a moment.

Jenny followed him into the dark living room. He clicked on a table lamp and turned to face her, his expression questioning. He was wearing a pale blue T-shirt over wrinkled tan shorts. He was barefoot.

"My parents went to bed early," he said softly, gesturing toward their room in back. "I was just listening to some music."

"I — I had to talk to you," Jenny told him, avoiding his stare. She sat down on the arm of the worn, brown leather couch. "I didn't want to do it over the phone."

His blue eyes locked on hers. The light caught the scar along the bottom of his chin. "What's going on?" he asked warily.

"Change of plans," she said softly.

She told him she was going to stay with her cousin upstate for the summer. At first, he didn't seem to react. He stared at her blankly with his pale blue eyes, rubbing the scar under his chin.

"Maybe I'll come with you," he said finally, dropping down on the couch and taking her hand. "I mean, I don't have a job yet. I could go with you and look for a summer job up there. Then we could be together."

Jenny squeezed his hand. "You know your

parents wouldn't let you do that," she said softly.

"Sure they would," he insisted. "They don't care what I do."

Jenny shook her head. "I — I've been so messed up, Cal. I really need a total change." She paused, watching his expression change to disappointment. "I'll be back in September," she whispered. "Then we can have fun catching up on all the good times we missed during the summer."

He let go of her hand and climbed to his feet. Then he walked slowly to the window and stared out at the darkness.

He's hurt, Jenny thought. He's really hurt.

He stared out into the dark night, leaning with both hands on the windowsill.

"Well . . . aren't you going to say anything?" she demanded finally.

She could see the muscles in his jaw tighten. "What's there to say?" he muttered bitterly. "You've already made up your mind. You're ruining our summer."

He's acting tough, Jenny thought, staring at his hard, cold expression. He doesn't want me to see how hurt he is. So he's acting hard and tough.

Or *is* he acting?

Staring across the room at him, she realized

she didn't know Cal very well. In fact, Jenny realized with a shudder, she didn't know him at all.

"Hi," Debra Jeffers whispered, "is this Terry?" She was lying on her back in her bed, the cordless phone cradled between her shoulder and chin.

"Yeah. Who's this?" Terry replied suspiciously on the other end of the line.

"Don't you know who it is?" Debra whispered, teasing. She giggled.

"No. Who is it?" Terry asked impatiently.

Debra could picture the bewildered look on his face as he tried to identify his mystery caller. She could imagine his green eyes narrowed in concentration, the little freckles flaring on his cheeks.

He's so cute, she thought.

"I've been watching you, Terry," she whispered sexily. "From afar."

"Come on," he groaned. "Give me a break. Is this Loren?"

Debra giggled. "No, Terry. Guess again."

"What do you want? I've got to go mow the lawn," he said.

"What do I want? I want *you!*" Debra whispered.

"Huh?"

"I want you, Terry."

"Who *is* this?" he demanded.

"Your secret admirer. Come on. Can't you guess?"

Silence.

"Don't you want to get to know me, Terry?" Debra teased.

He cleared his throat. "Do you want to go out or something?" he asked in a low voice.

"Do *you?*" Debra whispered.

"I guess," he replied reluctantly. "But who is this?"

"It's me," Debra whispered.

"Who's me?"

"I told you. I'm your secret admirer." She pushed herself up on the bed, crossing her long legs, staring up at her bedroom ceiling.

"Listen. I've got to go," Terry said.

"Don't go. I'll miss you, Terry," Debra teased.

"Do you . . . uh . . . want to go out tonight?" Terry asked.

Debra giggled. "What do you like to do at night, Terry?"

"Huh?"

"What would you like to do with *me* tonight?"

He snickered. "Whoever you are, you have a very sexy voice."

"Thank you, Terry," Debra whispered. "You do, too. Your voice really turns me on."

There was a long pause. "So do you want to go out?"

"I can't," she told him.

"Huh? Why not?"

"Because then I wouldn't be a secret admirer anymore, would I!"

Debra hung up and tossed the phone beside her on the bed.

Thinking about how confused Terry must be, she laughed out loud.

But her laughter was cut short when she saw the shadowy figure looming in the doorway.

"You!" Debra cried angrily, scrambling to her feet. "What are *you* doing here?"

# Chapter 4

The figure stepped out of the shadows. He stared at Debra in silence, his expression blank.

"Don — what are you doing here?" Debra demanded. Glaring at him angrily, she tossed her long blonde hair back over her shoulder with one hand.

"I want to talk to you," he replied, returning her stare.

He's so big, she thought. So powerfully built. Don was on the wrestling team at school. He worked out all the time.

It was one of the things that had attracted her to him the previous fall. She had never gone out with a real jock before.

He was wearing maroon sweats. His short, brown hair appeared wet, as if he had just showered.

He took another few steps toward her. His

expression turned menacing. His round, dark eyes burned into hers.

She felt a shudder of fear, but held her ground. "Who let you in? How long have you been standing there spying on me?" she demanded.

"Long enough." He picked up a small stuffed dog from her dressertop and examined it.

"Put that down," Debra snapped. "Get out of here, Don."

"I just want to talk," he said, shuffling the dog from hand to hand.

His hands are so big, he could crush that stuffed animal, Debra thought.

"There's nothing to talk about," she said coldly. She walked over and grabbed the stuffed dog from his hands.

His dark eyes narrowed in hurt. "No harm in talking, is there?"

"Don, please," Debra pleaded impatiently. "I really want you to leave. We broke up, okay? You're a great guy, but I don't want to go out with you anymore."

"But, Deb — "

"And I don't want you barging into my house, haunting me all the time." She tossed her long hair back again. It was constantly falling over her face, and she was constantly brushing it back over her shoulders.

"You're cold," Don said, his handsome face reddening. He shook his head. "You're really cold, Debra."

" 'Bye-'bye," she replied, motioning to the door.

"Maybe I'll tell Terry how cold you are," Don said, picking up another stuffed dog from her dressertop collection.

"Terry? What about Terry?" Debra snapped.

A dark grin spread across Don's face. "Maybe I'll tell Terry who his secret admirer is." He snickered.

"You mind your own business," Debra said sharply. "Just get out of my life, okay?"

"Maybe I'll tell Mark, too," Don threatened, tossing the dog from hand to hand. "Maybe I'll tell your boyfriend Mark how you like to call Terry at night and whisper to him over the phone."

"You pig!" Debra screamed angrily. She could feel herself losing control, but couldn't stop herself.

She had broken up with Don two weeks ago when school let out. What right did he have to be in her bedroom, listening to her private conversations, threatening to tell Mark, threatening to spoil her summer — out of childish spite?

"Get *out!*" she screamed, and threw the stuffed dog at him.

It bounced off his broad chest.

Don laughed. He strode forward and grabbed Debra's arm.

Then, with surprising strength, he pulled her to him, nearly lifting her off her feet.

He pushed his mouth against hers in a desperate kiss.

"Let go!" She struggled to free herself, pulling back with all her strength.

He laughed again, his dark eyes wild with excitement.

His hand tightened around her arm as he pulled her close again. "Debra, please — "

"Let go!" Debra shrieked. "Don — stop! Stop — you're *hurting* me! What are you going to do?"

# Chapter 5

"Don — stop!"

Debra struggled to squirm out of his grasp, but he was too strong.

"Hey — what's going on?" a voice called from the doorway.

Startled, Don released Debra and spun around.

"Jenny — !" Debra cried, grateful for the intrusion.

"I'm all unpacked," Jenny said, staring at Don. "I heard voices and — "

"This is Don. He was just leaving," Debra said brusquely, rubbing her arm where Don had gripped it.

"Hi," Don said to Jenny, embarrassed, his face bright red. "You're Debra's cousin?"

"Yes. Jenny Jeffers," Jenny told him, casting Debra a questioning glance.

"Same last name. As Debra," Don said awkwardly. He turned to Debra. "Hey, sorry. I didn't mean to hurt you or anything. I was just — "

" 'Bye," Debra said coldly. "Don't call me. I'll call you."

Don, his face still tomato-red, started to say something, but stopped. He shook his head regretfully, then turned and hurried from the room, the floorboards groaning under his heavy footsteps.

"What a creep," Debra declared after she and Jenny heard the front door slam behind him. "I can't believe I went out with him for the whole school year."

"Was he hurting you?" Jenny asked, concerned. "I heard you shouting and — "

"Don's just a big animal," Debra said, rubbing her arm. "But he's harmless." She snickered. "And he's history. He won't be coming back."

"The last time I was here, you were going with a little skinny guy named David," Jenny said. She bent to pick up a stuffed dog from the rug.

"That's old news," Debra told her, tossing back her hair. "Skinny David was at least three boyfriends ago."

"I'm impressed," Jenny said, and laughed.

"You'll like Mark," Debra said, taking the

stuffed dog and returning it to its place on the dressertop. "I've been going with him since I dumped Don. He's a great guy. You'll meet him later."

"I will?" Jenny asked.

Debra started to reply, but her mother appeared in the doorway. "Jenny, do you need anything? Can I help you unpack? Is your room okay? I love that top."

"This? It's just from the Gap," Jenny said.

Debra's mother, Julia Jeffers, always talked a mile a minute. She never asked one question when it was possible to ask three. She was a pretty, energetic woman, young-looking, with a boyish figure, her blonde hair cut in a short bob. She wore a blue Lycra tanktop over black leggings.

"We haven't seen you for so long," Mrs. Jeffers said, turning Debra's desk chair around and sitting on it backwards. "How long has it been? Two years? Longer? I really can't remember."

"More than a year," Jenny replied. "But you look exactly the same, Aunt Julia."

"Bull," Mrs. Jeffers replied. But she was obviously pleased by the compliment.

"To answer your questions," Jenny continued, "the room is perfect, and I unpacked all my stuff."

"You don't need more hangers?" Debra's mother asked, leaning her chin on the back of the desk chair. "Another blanket, maybe? No. You won't need another blanket. That room gets pretty hot. It's in the sun all day. In fact, maybe we should get you a fan. I'll ask Carl about it. Did you call your mother?"

Jenny nodded. "Yeah. I called her before I unpacked." She turned to Debra. "It was really nice of you to invite me. I mean — "

"We really wanted you to come," Mrs. Jeffers offered before Debra could reply. "You and Debra have always gotten along so well. And since neither of you have brothers or sisters, you only have each other. You can be sisters all summer."

"Mom — !" Debra looked embarrassed.

"Well, when your mother said you needed a change of scenery," Mrs. Jeffers continued, ignoring Debra's protest, "I told her right away she should send you up here. Get some good fresh air. Meet a lot of new friends. You'll forget your problems soon enough."

"Thanks, Aunt Julia. I know it's going to be great," Jenny said sincerely.

A breeze fluttered the curtains in front of the open window. Jenny jumped, startled by the sudden movement.

Debra chuckled. "Ghosts," she joked.

"I can see you're a bundle of nerves," Mrs. Jeffers said to Jenny. "Your mother was right. You do need a change."

"I — yes. I do," Jenny replied awkwardly.

Debra glanced at the desk clock. "Oh, wow!" she exclaimed, jumping up. "It's nearly eight. I'm going to be late."

"You promised Mrs. Wagner you'd be prompt," Debra's mother scolded. She climbed to her feet and pushed the desk chair back under the desk. "Better hurry. You taking Jenny with you?"

"Yeah. Sure," Debra replied. She moved to the mirror and hurriedly started to brush out her hair.

"Have a good time," Mrs. Jeffers said, flashing Jenny a warm smile. "I'll be up when you get back. Carl and I always stay up very late." She started out the door, then returned to give Jenny a long hug. "I'm so glad you're here," she said. Then she hurried downstairs.

"Where are we going? What are you almost late for?" Jenny asked, turning to Debra.

Debra was busily applying lip gloss to her mouth. "To my job."

"Huh? You have a job?"

"Yeah." Debra nodded, staring at Jenny's reflection in the mirror. "But it's no problem. You can come with me."

"What kind of job?" Jenny asked. She moved beside Debra and started to straighten her own hair.

"Baby-sitting," Debra replied.

"Huh?" Jenny froze.

"I baby-sit this adorable baby three nights a week," Debra told her. "Just a couple of blocks from here. Wait till you see him. He's the cutest thing."

"Well, I don't know . . ." Jenny said reluctantly. She suddenly felt cold all over. Her knees were trembling. Her heart was thudding.

"Come on." Debra turned out the dressing table light and took Jenny's arm. She started to tug her to the door. "The baby sleeps the whole time. It's perfect. You and I can talk for hours, really catch up on things."

"But, Debra — "

"Jenny, come on," Debra urged. "It'll be fun."

# Chapter 6

"Your mom is really great," Jenny said.

"She drives me crazy," Debra replied. "She asks a million questions and then doesn't wait for an answer. She talks so fast, you can't remember which question you're answering!"

Jenny laughed.

"My poor dad can never get a word in," Debra continued heatedly. "I don't remember what his voice sounds like!"

"Well, I still think she's terrific," Jenny insisted. "She's been so nice to me."

Debra scowled. "She likes you. But wait till she gets to know you!"

Jenny laughed.

They were walking the three blocks to Mrs. Wagner's house. It was a warm night. A pale half moon floated low over the roofs of the houses. The air smelled fresh and sweet.

It felt good to be walking with Debra, talking, walking through a new neighborhood. Maybe Mom was right, Jenny thought. Maybe a change of scene was just what I needed.

"You and your mom get along, don't you?" Jenny asked, watching a station wagon filled with kids roll by slowly.

"Most of the time," Debra replied. "But she's just in my face too much. I mean . . ." She paused, debating whether or not to finish what she had started to say. Then she continued in a whisper, "That's why I told her I baby-sit *three* nights a week."

Jenny stopped at the curb, her mouth open in surprise. "Huh? You mean you *don't* work three nights?"

Debra shook her head. Her blonde hair caught the pale moonlight. Her eyes lit up mischievously. "No. Only two nights. On the third night I go out with Mark. My mom doesn't really approve of Mark. Do you believe it?"

"How come?" Jenny asked.

They crossed the street. The houses on the next block were older, Jenny saw. And larger. With wide, tree-filled front lawns bordered by tall, carefully trimmed hedges.

"No good reason," Debra replied with some bitterness. "He got in trouble in school last year. A cheating thing. No big deal. It wasn't even Mark's idea."

"And so your mom — "

"She says he has a flawed character," Debra replied, frowning. And then she added angrily, "Well — who doesn't?"

"Aren't you afraid of getting caught?" Jenny asked, watching a fat jack rabbit scamper across the sidewalk and disappear into a hedge. "I mean, on the night you're supposed to be baby-sitting?"

Debra didn't answer at first. Then she muttered, "I really don't care."

A car rolled past slowly. The driver, a teen-ager with long hair, leaned his head out the window and grinned at them. "Hey, how's it going?" he called over the blare of heavy metal guitars from his car radio. "Need a lift?"

"Not from you!" Debra called.

The car squealed away with a burst of speed.

"Do you know him?" Jenny asked.

"No," Debra replied. "But I didn't like his car."

They both laughed.

"There's Mrs. Wagner's house," Debra said, pointing.

Jenny gazed up at the long, ramshackle house, redbrick with tall, shuttered windows. The hedge along the front had grown wild, over the sidewalk. The lawn looked as if it hadn't been mowed in weeks. Tall weeds poked up everywhere.

Debra caught the surprised expression on Jenny's face. "Mrs. Wagner and her husband were divorced a few months ago," she explained. "I don't think she's had much time to think about taking care of the yard."

The two girls made their way up the driveway, their sneakers crunching over the gravel.

Jenny suddenly felt all of her muscles tense. She had a heavy feeling in the pit of her stomach. Her throat tightened.

She took a deep breath and held it.

I'm not the baby-sitter, she told herself. There's nothing to be afraid of.

Debra is the baby-sitter.

I'm just here to keep her company.

Nothing is going to happen. Nothing *can* happen.

She let her breath out slowly. Her heart was pounding. The heavy feeling in her stomach refused to leave. Her legs felt as if they weighed a thousand pounds as she followed Debra onto the front stoop.

The front door opened before Debra had a chance to knock.

"Hi, Debra. You're late," Mrs. Wagner said fretfully. She pushed open the screen door. The top of the screen was torn. It flapped loose from the frame.

"Sorry," Debra said quickly. "This is my cousin Jenny. She's visiting for the summer."

"Hi, Jenny," Mrs. Wagner said, biting her lower lip, studying Jenny quickly with her eyes.

Jenny suddenly realized she was still holding her breath. She let it out with a burst. "Nice to meet you," she choked out.

I don't want to be here, she thought, looking around the cluttered living room.

I don't want to baby-sit.

Something terrible will happen.

Something even more terrible than before will happen.

*You're not the baby-sitter!* she reminded herself. *Debra is the baby-sitter. Everything will be okay.*

Mrs. Wagner strode quickly to a low table and began shuffling through a bulging briefcase. "Got to make sure my assignment is here," she said. "I can't go to class without my assignment. Oh. Here it is."

Jenny stood awkwardly in the living room doorway, watching Mrs. Wagner. She was a thin, birdlike woman with a short mop of curly black hair, streaked with gray. Her green eyes darted nervously. She continued to bite her lower lip anxiously as she closed up the briefcase.

She wore black leggings that emphasized her skinny legs, and an oversized white shirt.

"You'd think I was going to Harvard or Yale instead of the community college," she said, straightening the collar of her shirt in the front entryway mirror. "But I do want to do well in this course."

She tucked the briefcase under her arm and turned to Debra. "Don't get married too early," she told her. "That's what I did. I never got to finish college. So now I have to do it two nights a week." She headed to the front door.

"Is Peter asleep?" Debra called after her.

"Oh. Peter. Of course. Yes." Mrs. Wagner shook her head. "I'm so nervous about this class, I forgot all about Peter. I'm a great mom, huh?"

"That's okay, Mrs. Wagner," Debra said, making her way to the stairs. "I'll go up and take a look at him. Don't worry. Peter's never any trouble at all."

"See you in a few hours," Mrs. Wagner said, and disappeared out the door. The screen door closed quietly behind her.

Debra turned to Jenny, a grin on her face. "She's a little nervous."

"I guess!" Jenny replied. "Let's go up and see Peter."

The baby was snoring softly, lying on his stomach. He had a mop of curly black hair, like his mother.

"He's a good sleeper," Debra whispered, reaching over the side of the crib to straighten his light blanket. "Usually he doesn't wake up at all when I'm here."

"What an easy job," Jenny whispered back.

They tiptoed back downstairs, got Cokes from the refrigerator, and settled down across from each other in big living room armchairs.

Jenny gazed around the room. The furniture was big and comfortable-looking. But every surface — the tabletops, the bookshelves, the window ledges — was cluttered with objects of all kinds: small glass vases, porcelain figurines, tiny picture frames with old photographs inside them, china eggs, miniature soldiers, painted thimbles.

"I guess Mrs. Wagner is a collector," Jenny said, picking up a tiny china pitcher. It felt cool and smooth in her hand.

"Do you believe all this *stuff?*" Debra replied, shaking her head. Then she startled Jenny by jumping to her feet, nearly knocking over an end table filled with tiny animal figurines. "The signal! I almost forgot!"

"Huh? What signal?"

Debra hurried out of the room. She returned a few seconds later. "I had to make sure the porch light was on. That's our signal. If the light is on, Mark knows it's safe to come in."

Jenny set down her Coke can. "Mark? He's coming here?"

"Yeah. He usually comes about half an hour after Mrs. Wagner leaves. Unless the porch light is off." Debra took a long sip of Coke. "You'll like Mark. He's really great," she said, tossing her hair behind her shoulders.

A loud click, probably the refrigerator turning on in the kitchen, made Jenny jump. "Sorry," she told Debra. "I — I'm a little jumpy. I mean, baby-sitting. You know."

Debra gasped. "Oh, Jenny. I'm so sorry. I completely forgot — "

Jenny shook her head and forced a smile. "No. I'll be okay. Really. I — I have to get over this. I can't just live in constant fear, you know?"

Debra studied her face. "I never really heard the whole story," she said softly. "I mean, about what happened to you. Can you talk about it? Is it hard for you?"

Jenny's hand tightened around the Coke can.

She tucked her legs under her on the chair cushion. She cleared her throat. "There isn't much to tell, really."

"I know you went through something terrible," Debra said, staring down at a worn spot in the carpet.

"Yeah. Terrible," Jenny repeated. "I had a job, see. Baby-sitting for this family. The Hagens. They had this really cute little boy. Donny." Jenny sighed.

"Listen, if you don't want to tell me . . ." Debra started.

"After I baby-sat for Donny for a while, I started getting these frightening phone calls," Jenny continued, staring hard at the red-and-white can until it became a blur. "A whispered voice saying, *'Are you all alone, Babes? Company's coming.'*"

"Yuck," Debra said, pulling up her legs and sitting sideways in the big armchair.

"There had been all these attacks on baby-sitters all over town." Jenny continued. "And here I was, getting these frightening calls, getting these threats. And then . . . and then . . ."

She took a deep breath. "It turned out that Mr. Hagen, Donny's dad, he was the one making the calls. He was the one attacking the baby-sitters."

"But why?" Debra asked.

"He and his wife had a baby. And the baby died when a baby-sitter was taking care of it. And I guess Mr. Hagen just freaked. He started murdering baby-sitters all over town."

"I don't believe it!" Debra cried with a shiver. "It — it's like a horror movie."

Jenny nodded. She realized her hands were shaking. She set the Coke can down on the end table. "No one knew who was attacking the baby-sitters. The police couldn't catch the guy. But one night I figured out it was Mr. Hagen," she told Debra, speaking in a low whisper. "That night, I thought he was driving me home. But he knew that I knew. He drove me to this deserted rock quarry outside of town. A deep hole with nothing but rocks down below. He backed me up to the edge."

"He was going to push you over the side?" Debra cried, her face pale with horror. She tugged at a strand of blonde hair, twisting it in her fingers.

"Yes," Jenny said. She cleared her throat again. "He came running to me to push me over. But I ducked. He — he sailed over the edge. He fell. Onto the rocks. I — I heard his body crack. It sounded just like an egg cracking. I can still hear that sound. Still."

"Wow," Debra exclaimed, tugging at her

hair. "Wow." She raised her eyes to Jenny. "He was killed?"

Jenny nodded. "I know it wasn't really my fault. I mean, Mr. Hagen was evil. He was a crazy, evil man. He deserved to die. But I can't stop thinking about him. I can't stop thinking it was my fault."

"But he was a killer, Jenny," Debra said. "You have to keep telling yourself that. You can't feel guilty. He was a killer."

"After Mr. Hagen died, I started getting calls from him," Jenny revealed. "The same threats. The same whispered threats: *'Company's coming, Babes.'*"

Debra sat up. Her mouth dropped open. "What do you mean? How could you get calls from him after he died?"

"I was baby-sitting for another family," Jenny explained. "A little boy named Eli. And the calls started. The threats started. I — I really thought Mr. Hagen had come back. That he was back from the grave. Or that maybe he really hadn't died at all. I — I started having these frightening nightmares about him coming back, coming back to get me. I still have them."

Debra shuddered. "You poor thing. But he was definitely dead, right?"

Jenny nodded. "It was someone else. It was my doctor's assistant. She was jealous of me.

So she pretended to be Mr. Hagen. She made the frightening calls. She frightened me so much. It was so cruel. So cruel."

"That is really *sick!*" Debra exclaimed.

"I've been seeing Dr. Schindler for nearly two years," Jenny revealed, shifting her position in the big chair. "He says I'm doing really well, making a lot of progress. But I'm not so sure." Her voice trailed off. She stared down at the carpet.

"Why? What's wrong?" Debra asked.

"I still have the nightmares," Jenny replied. "I still dream about Mr. Hagen. I still see him pulling himself up from his grave, half-decayed, chunks of skin falling off his face."

"Wow," Debra muttered, twisting her hair around her finger, staring sympathetically at her cousin.

"And I think I see him wherever I go," Jenny admitted. She shuddered. She tried to continue, but no sound came out. She took a long drink from the Coke can.

"Maybe I shouldn't have brought you here," Debra said thoughtfully. "Maybe baby-sitting brings back too many horrible memories for you."

"No. I'll be okay," Jenny assured her. "It's good for me, I think. I mean, I should face my fears. I guess. It's just that . . ." She sighed.

"Just what?" Debra asked softly.

"I have this weird feeling," Jenny replied after a while. "This sick feeling that Mr. Hagen *is* still alive. That's why I can't stop dreaming about him. Seeing him. Because he *is* still alive. He *is* going to come for me."

"Jenny, no," Debra said. She climbed to her feet and moved next to Jenny's chair. She put a comforting hand on Jenny's shoulder. "You saw him die, Jenny. He's dead. That's it. You have to stop thinking like that. You have to stop thinking about this creep Mr. Hagen. You have to put it all behind you."

"I — I don't think I can," Jenny confessed.

Another noise in the kitchen made them both jump. Debra squeezed Jenny's shoulder.

"What was that?" Debra whispered.

They froze, listening.

A scraping sound.

A creaking floorboard.

Footsteps.

A cough.

"Debra — someone's in the house," Jenny whispered.

# Chapter 7

They both heard another harsh cough from the kitchen.

More scraping of shoes against the floor.

Jenny climbed to her feet, her features tight with fear. Debra stood beside her, still as a statue, listening hard.

"Is it Mark?" Jenny whispered.

Debra shook her head. "He wouldn't come in the back."

"Let's call the police," Jenny suggested, her voice a trembling whisper.

Debra swallowed hard, her eyes wide with terror. "The phone's in the kitchen."

"Huh?" Jenny reacted with shock. "Deb, there's got to be another phone."

"No. Mrs. Wagner had to cut back when her husband left."

Without realizing it, the girls had begun to make their way to the kitchen. Keeping against

the hallway wall, they crept silently, Debra
leading the way, their eyes on the yellow rectangle of light from the kitchen.

They stopped just outside the kitchen door.

Jenny leaned hard against the wall. She felt
dizzy. The floor had started to tilt. The flow-
ered hallway wallpaper became a shimmering
blur.

What am I doing here? she thought, closing
her eyes, trying to force her heart to stop thudding so hard in her chest.

Why am I baby-sitting again?

Why are frightening things happening to me
again?

When she opened her eyes, she saw that
Debra had stepped into the kitchen. "Who's
there?" Debra called loudly. "Who is it?" Her
voice trembled, revealing her fear.

Jenny took a hesitant step forward, determined to keep up with her cousin.

"Who's there?" Debra repeated shrilly.

"*I'm back!*" a strange voice replied.

# Chapter 8

*"He can't be back!"*

Jenny wasn't sure whether she thought the words or screamed them.

*"He can't be back! He's dead!"*

Debra turned to stare at her. Her hands pressed against her face, Jenny stepped into the kitchen — and saw a large, brightly dressed woman staring back at her from the sink.

"I'm back," the woman repeated in a hoarse, throaty voice. She narrowed her dark eyes at the two startled girls, as if challenging them.

The woman appeared to Jenny to be somewhere between fifty and sixty. She was short and very fat. She wore an enormous, flower-patterned wraparound skirt and a bright yellow sweater. Her face was heavily made up, with heavy black eyebrows painted above her dark eyes, and thick red lipstick smeared over her mouth. Her round cheeks were pink. She had raven-black hair pulled straight back into a long ponytail.

Standing at the sink, she carried a plain brown shopping bag in one pudgy hand. Her fingers were covered with sparkly rings, Jenny saw.

"I came back," she repeated, still squinting at Jenny and Debra, her expression menacing.

"Who *are* you?" Debra managed to say.

"Maggie," she replied. "And I haven't been drinking, if that's your next question."

"But how did you get in?" Debra asked, flashing a quick glance at Jenny.

Jenny located the wallphone beside the kitchen counter. It would be easy to reach it quickly, she decided, to call the police.

"I still have my key," Maggie said, a smile crossing her bright lips. "Mrs. Wagner forgot to take back my key."

Debra relaxed a little. "You work for Mrs. Wagner?"

"Used to," the woman said. She made a disgusted face. "I was the housekeeper. But I was . . . how do you say it? . . . let go."

"But you — " Debra started.

"I never drank during the day," Maggie interrupted, staring hard at Debra as if expecting her to challenge the statement. "And I certain'y never drank when I took care of little Peter."

Debra flashed another worried glance at Jenny.

"Things disappeared," Maggie said. She reached up her free hand and turned on the sink faucet, then quickly turned it off. "Things disappeared around here. Mrs. Wagner's husband disappeared, didn't he!" She threw back her head and laughed, a deep, throaty laugh. "Yeah. The husband disappeared. Then poor Maggie had to disappear."

*She's crazy.* Debra mouthed the words to Jenny.

Jenny nodded in reply, her expression troubled.

"Things disappeared certain'y. But I didn't disappear 'em," Maggie said with increasing anger. She turned the faucet on and off again. "I didn't disappear 'em, you hear?"

"Yes," Debra muttered, watching the woman turn the faucet on and off, on and off.

"You can't just turn Maggie off like a faucet," the woman said, saying each word slowly and distinctly.

Debra took a deep breath and stepped closer to Maggie. "Well, I'm the baby-sitter tonight," she said. "Can I help you or anything?"

"I'm only taking this bag," the woman said,

holding up the empty shopping bag. "I'm only taking what's certain'y mine."

"That's fine," Debra said shakily.

"Fine," Maggie repeated. "Fine, fine, fine!" The word sounded angrier with each repetition. "I'll tell *you* what's fine, young lady!" she shouted.

"Maggie, please — " Debra pleaded.

"Fine, fine, fine!" Maggie shook a fat fist at Debra. "I know what's fine and what's not. I certain'y never drank during the day."

"That's good," Debra said, her voice unsteady.

"Certain'y things disappeared. But I didn't disappear 'em. I didn't disappear Mr. Wagner!" Again, she had a hearty laugh at her private joke.

"Well, shall I tell Mrs. Wagner you were here?" Debra asked.

Maggie cut her laughter short. "I only came for what's mine." She held up the brown shopping bag. "That's all I want. What's mine. You can't turn Maggie off like a faucet. I want what's mine."

She started to the kitchen door, swaying heavily from side to side as she walked, folding the shopping bag under the arm of her yellow sweater.

"Well, good night," Debra called after her, relief in her voice.

Maggie turned at the door. Her eyes narrowed. Her expression turned hard. "Stay away from here!" she shouted, spitting the words.

"Huh?" Debra cried, startled by the woman's sudden threat.

"Stay away from here," Maggie repeated. "It isn't the place for you. Things disappear. You hear me? Things disappear."

The screen door slammed hard behind her.

As soon as she was gone, Debra slumped against the kitchen counter and collapsed in laughter. "Do you believe her?" she cried. "Do you believe her? And what was she wearing — a beach umbrella?"

"I thought she was kind of scary," Jenny said softly, her arms crossed over her chest. "She was so drunk."

"Drunk and crazy," Debra said, shaking her head.

"She seemed so angry," Jenny said thoughtfully, staring at the darkness beyond the screen door. "I mean, she was threatening us there before she left, wasn't she?"

"She's messed up," Debra said, shaking her head. "She's *way* messed up. We'll have to tell

Mrs. Wagner to get the locks changed."

With a shiver, Jenny started to make her way back toward the living room. "I was scared," she admitted. "Really scared."

"Me, too," Debra replied. "At first, anyway."

"I — I thought it was Mr. Hagen," Jenny confessed softly. "Isn't that awful? That was the first thing I thought. It's Mr. Hagen. He's back. He's followed me here." Her voice cracked with emotion. "Am I crazy, Debra? Am I totally crazy?"

"Of course not," Debra replied soothingly. "Just stop thinking about Mr. Hagen, Jenny. Tell yourself you're going to stop thinking about him. From this moment on."

"Yes. You're right. I have to do that," Jenny said uncertainly. "He's never coming back. Never."

And then both girls cried out in alarm at the sound of the heavy pounding on the front door.

# Chapter 9

The knocking was repeated. Even louder.

Jenny stared at the door but didn't move.

Debra started to laugh. "It's only Mark," she said, putting a comforting hand on Jenny's shoulder. She hurried down the hall and pulled open the door.

"Hey, didn't you hear me knocking? I've been out here for ten minutes!" Mark declared. He pushed past Debra into the hallway, an annoyed frown on his face.

His expression turned to surprise when he saw Jenny. "Oh. Hi."

He was good-looking, Jenny instantly decided. He had wavy red-brown hair with sideburns that framed his slender face. He had obviously spent a lot of time outdoors, for he had a dark suntan, even though it was only June. The tan made his green eyes sparkle like emeralds. He wore faded blue denim jeans and a sleeveless navy-blue T-shirt.

"We were back in the kitchen. Why didn't you ring the bell?" Debra asked.

"You're Jenny — right?" Mark asked, ignoring Debra's question.

Jenny nodded. "Yes. Hi, Mark."

"I guess Debra has told you a lot about me," he said playfully. "Well, it's all true."

"I never mentioned your name," Debra said dryly. She punched his bare shoulder. "You're so tanned, you're disgusting."

"Hey, thanks," he replied, grabbing her hand before she could punch him again. "You're cute, too."

They wandered into the living room. Debra sat beside Mark on the couch. Jenny eased into the big armchair across from them, sliding her legs onto the arm. "How'd you get so tan?" she asked Mark.

"I'm a lifeguard," he told her. "At the community pool."

"All the twelve-year-old girls love him," Debra said, squeezing his hand. "They pretend to drown so Mark can save them."

"Do you save them?" Jenny asked, laughing.

"Only the cute ones," Mark replied.

"You're a pig," Debra told him, rolling her eyes. "A disgusting tanned pig."

"You're so nice tonight," Mark said sarcastically. He put his hands around Debra's throat and playfully pretended to strangle her.

"Is it a fun job?" Jenny asked when they stopped wrestling. "Being a lifeguard?"

"Kind of," Mark replied thoughtfully, scratching his chest through the blue T-shirt. "Mostly you just sit there. It's almost like watching TV. Except you get to blow a whistle a lot."

"Mark's very deep," Debra said sarcastically.

They all laughed. Debra snuggled against Mark.

"Wish I had a summer job," Jenny said wistfully.

Debra reacted with surprise. "You do? I thought you just wanted to chill out this summer."

"Not really," Jenny told her. "I had a job back home. Before you invited me to come here. I'm really going to need some money in the fall. You know. For clothes and school stuff. And with Mom laid off . . ."

"I'll bet my dad could get you a job," Mark offered. He slid his arm around Debra's shoulders.

"You do?" Jenny shifted in the chair, lowering her feet to the floor.

"Yeah," Mark told her. "Dad's best friend owns the riding stable up on Clearlake Road. He's always looking for helpers in the summer."

"You mean horseback riding teachers?" Jenny asked. "I used to be a good rider."

"No. Just helpers," Mark said. "You know. Wranglers, they call them. They get a lot of day campers up there. Little kids riding. They need people to help them up on their horses and show them how to put their feet in the stirrups. You know. Stuff like that."

"And people to catch them when they fall on their heads!" Debra joked.

Mark laughed and pulled Debra close. "You're sick," he said. "You're really sick."

"You say the sweetest things," Debra replied.

"I guess I could do that," Jenny told Mark with growing enthusiasm. "I mean, be a wrangler. That could be fun."

"I'll talk to my dad tomorrow," Mark promised. And then his eyes opened wide with surprise and he leapt to his feet as bright yellow headlights rolled up the living room wall.

They heard the rumble of a car outside.

"Mrs. Wagner is home early!" Mark declared.

"Quick — get *out* of here!" Debra cried, giving him a shove.

Mark stumbled over the low coffee table, knocking over several china knickknacks. "Ow!" he cried out, but kept running toward the back door.

Debra hurried to the large living room window and peered out.

"Won't Mrs. Wagner see his car?" Jenny asked.

"Wait!" Debra called. "Mark — wait!"

"Huh? What's wrong?" Mark's shout came from the kitchen.

"It's not her," Debra called. "It's just a car turning around in the drive." She laughed.

A few seconds later, Mark returned, rubbing the knee that had hit the table. "Heart attack time," he said breathlessly, grinning at Jenny.

"Does this happen often?" Jenny asked.

"Only once a night," Debra replied, motioning for Mark to come back to his place beside her on the couch.

Mark glanced at his watch. "I'll have to go soon. She'll be back in half an hour or so."

Debra pulled him close and they began kissing.

Jenny looked away. *Three's company*, she told herself.

But what was she supposed to do while they were making out?

She climbed out of the chair and explored the room, picking up china figurines, studying the dozens of snapshots in multicolored frames.

Debra and Mark have forgotten I'm here, she thought, rolling her eyes. She took a quick glance at them, totally entwined on the couch.

She decided to wander upstairs and take another look at Peter.

A few minutes later, Debra sighed and pulled her face from Mark's. She took a couple of breaths. Then, smiling, started to lean forward to kiss him again.

But Jenny's terrified scream made Debra pull back.

"Debra — help! Come quick! The baby — he isn't breathing!"

# Chapter 10

"Debra — quick! *Please!*"

Jenny's shrill, terrified cry made Debra gasp. She pushed herself up and plunged toward the stairway, Mark right behind her.

This can't be happening, Debra thought, feeling sick.

It *can't!*

It seemed to take an eternity to climb the stairs. She reached the landing, panting loudly.

"Debra — the baby!"

Debra hesitated just outside the baby's door, swallowing hard. Then she burst into the room.

In the dim light from the nightlight on the floor, Debra saw Jenny huddled over the crib. Jenny looked up as Debra and Mark entered, her features twisted in horror, her chin trembling.

"He — he's — "

Debra took a deep breath, stepped up beside

Jenny, and bent over the crib. The baby was silent.

So deadly silent.

With a trembling hand, she touched his face.

Still warm.

She slid her hands under his arms and lifted him up.

He opened his eyes.

He gurgled his surprise at being awakened.

"Oh!" Jenny sank back against the wall, her hands raised to her face. Debra could see that she was trembling all over.

"He's fine," Debra told her, her voice a trembling whisper.

"Oh, man!" Mark cried. "What a scare!" He sank to his knees.

"You're fine, aren't you, Peter?" Debra asked the baby, pressing her forehead against his. She held him against her for a long moment, then lowered him to his crib.

He made a few noises, then settled back to sleep.

Debra raised her eyes accusingly to Jenny.

"He — he was so quiet," Jenny stammered, tears rolling down her cheeks. "He'd been snoring before. But then he was so totally silent, and it's so dark in here, I — "

"Wow," Mark repeated, still on his knees on the shaggy carpet. "Wow."

Debra walked over to Jenny and put a comforting arm around her trembling shoulders. "You really *are* a nervous thing, aren't you," she said softly.

"I'm sorry," Jenny said. "I'm really sorry."

"No. I'm sorry," Debra replied, still holding her. "I forced you to come here tonight. I shouldn't have."

Jenny apologized again, wiping tears off her cheeks with her hands. "I — I really lost it, Debra. I feel so stupid."

"You were scared, that's all," Debra replied. She led the way back downstairs.

"I feel like a perfect jerk," Jenny muttered, shaking her head.

"Stop," Debra told her. "No one's perfect."

Jenny forced a smile. But her thoughts were dark and painful.

What's *wrong* with me? she wondered.

Will I *ever* get over this? Am I totally cracking up?

"Now, where *were* we?" Mark asked slyly, pulling Debra back to the couch.

But once again, headlights rolled up over the wallpaper.

"Mrs. Wagner!" Debra cried. " 'Bye, Mark!"

" 'Bye, guys!" Once again, Mark went flying to the kitchen.

Jenny checked her face in the hallway mirror, making sure she had wiped away all traces of tears.

The kitchen door slammed. The front door opened. Mrs. Wagner entered, carrying her bulging briefcase. "How'd it go, girls?" she asked.

"Just fine," Debra told her brightly. "No problem."

"Hey, this is great!" the boy said, grinning down at Jenny. He rustled the reins in front of him. His horse, a brown mare with white markings on its legs, brushed a fly off its hind quarters with a swish of its tail.

"Hold still," Jenny said. "Let me adjust the stirrups for you, Brad." She tugged the stirrup strap tighter, then slid the boy's foot into it. "How's that feel?" she asked.

"Perfect," Brad replied.

Jenny slapped some dust off the leg of her jeans, then smiled up at him. Just three days at this job, she thought, and already I'm a pro.

The horse snorted as if reading her thoughts.

"Just remember, Brad," Jenny instructed, leading the horse over to the others in Brad's day camp group, "pull back hard on the reins, and your horse will stop. But as soon as she stops, stop tugging. Or else the horse will think you want to back up. Got it?"

"Got it," Brad assured her. He called to a friend, "Hey, look — this is easy!" The horse walked slowly over the dusty path. "What's my horse's name?" the boy called back to Jenny.

"Pockets," she shouted.

"Pockets?"

Jenny watched him pull back on the reins. The horse obediently stopped. He's a cute kid, she thought.

She untied another horse, a black gelding, from the hitching post. "Who's next?" she called.

A timid-looking girl with long, copper-colored hair stepped forward slowly.

"Come on," Jenny beckoned encouragingly. "I've got a nice, gentle horse for you."

A few minutes later, the twelve kids in the day camp group and their counselor were riding off on the dirt trail that led through the woods, their horses loping slowly, a riding instructor in the front and one at the rear.

Jenny watched until they disappeared into the trees. Then she started to the stable to get a water bucket.

"Hey, how's it going?" A voice right behind her.

Jenny turned to see Gary Killeen smiling at her. He wiped his forehead with the red bandanna he wore around his neck. Then he replaced his battered black Stetson hat on his head.

Gary was nineteen or twenty. He was a real wrangler. From Jackson Hole, Wyoming.

He wasn't exactly handsome, but Jenny liked the way he looked. He had thick, golden eyebrows that looked like big caterpillars under his cowboy hat. His eyes were steely gray, narrow and close together. He had a great smile, Jenny thought, with two front teeth that jutted out at odd angles.

"I'm doing great," she told him, slowing her pace so he could catch up with her. He had been really friendly to her since her first day, and had shown her a lot about saddles and stirrups and the other equipment.

"The kids really seem to like you," Gary said, lowering the brim of his hat.

"Well, I used to . . . uh . . . be a baby-sitter," she told him.

"I used to be a baby," he said, grinning at her, his gray eyes lighting up under the thick, blond eyebrows.

He has a weird sense of humor, she thought.

"Not too busy today," she said. They stepped into the shade of the stable. Jenny took a deep breath. The air smelled of hay and horse sweat.

"Busy enough," Gary replied. "We got another camp group this afternoon."

"How many?" Jenny asked, filling the water bucket.

"Fourteen, I think." Gary stood with his hands on the hips of his straight-legged jeans, admiring her as if she were a prize stallion.

Jenny could feel herself blushing. "I'll help you saddle up the horses," she offered.

"You *bet* you will!" he exclaimed, chuckling. "You know, you're not a bad-looking filly yourself," he said, lowering his eyes to his boots.

"Thanks. I guess," Jenny replied awkwardly. She hoisted the bucket, water slopping over the sides. "I've got to go water Betsy and Jedediah."

"Who *names* these horses?" Gary exclaimed, shaking his head.

Jenny tended to Betsy and Jedediah. The horses seemed so tranquil, standing under the hot sun, chewing at some grass, waiting for their next assignment.

Jenny stroked Betsy's mane for a while. The horse uttered a low whinny in appreciation, then kept on pulling up slender weeds from the dirt.

When she returned the bucket to the stable, she looked for Gary. But he had disappeared. Probably in the small office behind the stable.

It was so quiet, so calm.

Jenny leaned against the rail fence in front

of the stable, staring out at the green woods, waiting for the day camp group to return.

After a while, she found herself thinking about Cal. He had promised he'd write. But she'd been up here more than a week, and hadn't heard a word from him.

I wonder what he's doing right this minute, she thought. I wonder if he's thinking about me. I wonder if he found a job. I wonder if he's going to come up here to visit me.

Maybe I'll phone him tonight, she thought.

Debra popped into her mind. The night before, Debra had been playing one of her telephone pranks. She had called a boy named Terry and whispered sexy things to him, telling him she was his secret admirer.

Jenny listened in on an extension. Terry got all tongue-tied and then tried to persuade his "secret admirer" to go out with him. Debra hung up on him while he was still talking.

Jenny thought the whole thing was kind of cruel, but she and Debra giggled the rest of the night about it.

Debra admitted she had a real crush on Terry.

"Does Mark know?" Jenny had asked.

"Of course not," Debra exclaimed. "And he'd better never find out. Mark seems like a quiet kind of guy, but he can get really jealous."

Leaning against the fence, letting the sun beat down on her face, Jenny remembered the night before and allowed herself a few envious thoughts about Debra.

Everything comes so easily to Debra, she thought.

One boyfriend right after another.

Debra is such a secure person. She's so lucky.

She was still leaning against the fence rail, thinking about Debra, when the solitary rider came into view. He was approaching slowly along the path from the woods, his horse plodding, head down.

Jenny didn't remember saddling up a solitary rider this morning. Gary must have taken care of him, she thought, watching the man slowly move nearer, his feet pushing the stirrups out over the flanks of the black horse he rode.

The stable didn't get many solitary riders, especially in the morning. People usually rode in couples or groups.

Closer, the rider came. Into clear focus now.

Jenny recognized the horse. James.

What a stupid name for a horse, she thought.

Gary's right. The horses at this stable all have weird names.

As the horse drew nearer, Jenny could hear

the steady *clop-clop-clop* of its hooves on the dirt.

Shielding her eyes from the glare of the sun with one hand, she gazed at the rider.

He was a big man, very broad, wearing a red flannel shirt and gray slacks.

He had close-cropped brown hair that picked up the light of the sun. His face was very red.

He pulled up on the reins as the horse stepped up to the fence directly in front of Jenny. Steadying the horse, he stared down at Jenny with cold, steely-gray eyes.

His forehead was beaded with perspiration. His mouth was twisted in a crooked smile.

He leaned forward over the horse's neck.

Jenny stared up at him, her eyes locked on his cold gray eyes.

"Hi. I'm back," he said in a rough, gravelly voice.

Jenny stared wide-eyed into Mr. Hagen's face.

Then she opened her mouth and started to scream.

# Chapter 11

The next evening, Debra paced back and forth across her room, holding the cordless phone to her ear as she talked to Mark.

The curtains at the window fluttered and flapped in a stiff breeze. Outside, she could see a tiny patch of blue sky between heavy, dark rainclouds. It had rained hard all day.

"I guess Jenny is okay today," she told Mark, lowering her voice in case her cousin was nearby. "She hasn't come home from the stable yet."

"But what happened to her yesterday?" Mark asked.

Debra stared out the window at the widening patch of blue sky. "She freaked out. Just totally freaked," she replied.

"Huh? What do you mean?" Mark sounded confused.

"She thought she saw that man who died.

Mr. Hagen. I told you the whole story, Mark. Jenny keeps seeing him everywhere."

"You mean she thinks he's still alive?" Mark asked.

"I don't know," Debra said, glancing at the bedroom doorway. "I think Jenny thinks Mr. Hagen is coming back from the grave or something. She's really obsessed."

"Weird," Mark said softly. "So what happened at the stable?"

"Some guy rides up, and Jenny thinks he's Mr. Hagen. So she starts to scream. She screamed so loud, the poor guy nearly fell off his horse. I guess it took them a long time to calm her down."

"Wow," Mark exclaimed. "That's terrible."

"Jenny told me that afterwards she felt like a total jerk. She was so embarrassed. But she really couldn't help herself. She really thought the guy on the horse was Mr. Hagen."

"So then she went back to the stable this morning?" Mark asked.

"Yeah." Debra glanced again at the door. She thought she heard voices in the hall. "Jenny says she likes the job. I just hope she can keep herself together. She — "

Jenny entered the room, greeting Debra with a wave.

"I've got to go, Mark," Debra said into the

phone, smiling at Jenny. "Jenny just got home."

"Okay. Later," Mark replied.

"Hey, I'm baby-sitting at Mrs. Wagner's tonight," Debra added. "Are you going to come by? The usual time?"

"I can't," Mark said after a short pause. "I have to go somewhere with my dad."

Debra uttered a disappointed groan. "Are you sure you can't come?"

Mark said he was sure. They said good-bye.

"So how'd it go today? You get drenched?" Debra asked Jenny, setting the phone down on her dressertop.

"It was okay," Jenny said, picking up a string of brightly colored beads from Debra's dressing table. "We stayed in the stable, mostly. It was kind of boring. No one wants to ride horses in the rain."

"So what'd you do all day? Just feed the horses and clean up and stuff?"

Jenny slipped the beads around her neck and bent to admire herself in the dressing table mirror. "Yeah. And talked to Gary."

Debra's eyes widened with interest. "Gary? Who's Gary?"

"He's one of the wranglers," Jenny replied, adjusting the beads around her neck. "These are pretty. Where'd you get them?"

"Some guy gave them to me," Debra replied. "Don, I think. They're just plastic."

"But they're pretty," Jenny said, slipping them over her head, then examining them between her hands.

"And you felt okay today?" Debra asked sympathetically.

Jenny nodded. "Fine. No problem." She set the beads down on the dressing table, then bent to straighten her dark hair with her hand. "I'm a mess. I should take a shower. You're baby-sitting tonight?"

"Yeah. In a little while. Mrs. Wagner called to make sure I come on time tonight. She has an exam in her course. She was so pumped up about it, she could barely speak."

"Nice to know I'm not the only nervous person in the world," Jenny said dryly.

Debra suddenly had a devilish smile on her face. "I was thinking of giving Terry a little call before I go," she said.

"Poor Terry," Jenny replied, snickering.

"I think he'll be disappointed if he doesn't hear from me," Debra said, picking up the cordless phone. "I think he's starting to really enjoy having a secret admirer."

Jenny sat down on the edge of the bed. "Aren't you afraid he's going to recognize your voice?"

Debra thought about it for a long moment. Then her smile grew wider. "No. Not too afraid."

They both laughed.

"I have to admit, I get pretty turned on by these calls," Debra said. "What does that say about me?"

"That you're totally sick," Jenny replied, teasing.

Debra raised the phone and started to push Terry's number. But she suddenly stopped halfway through it. "Hey, I've got an idea."

"Uh-oh," Jenny replied, rolling her eyes.

Debra held the phone out to her cousin. "You do it."

Jenny's mouth dropped open. "Huh?"

"You make the call," Debra insisted, waving the phone in Jenny's face.

Jenny made no attempt to take it from her. "Me? Why?"

"Because it'll be funny," Debra replied. "And it'll totally mess him up."

"I can't!" Jenny cried.

"Take it. Take it." Debra shoved the phone in Jenny's face.

Jenny had no choice. She took the phone. "I can't. Really, Debra," she pleaded. "What should I say?"

"You'll think of something," Debra said,

grinning. "Just whisper sweet nothings in his ear. It's fun. You'll see. And you'll probably get turned on by it, too."

"Oh, yeah. Big thrill," Jenny said sarcastically. She sighed. "Okay, Deb. What's Terry's number?"

Debra told her the number. Then she sat down beside Jenny as Jenny dialed. "Don't be nervous," Debra instructed.

Jenny frowned. "I'm not nervous. I just think this is stu — " She stopped abruptly. Her voice changed to a sexy whisper. "Hello, Terry?"

"Yeah," Terry sounded immediately suspicious.

"Hi, Terry," Jenny whispered. "You don't know me, but I've been watching you."

Jenny glanced at Debra. Debra covered her mouth with her hand to suppress her giggles.

"Who is this? Is this Debra?" Terry demanded.

"Huh?" Jenny nearly dropped the phone.

"Debra, I know it's you," Terry said triumphantly.

"No, it's not Debra," Jenny uttered in her sexiest whisper. "I don't know anyone named Debra. Let's not talk about other girls, Terry. I just want to talk about you and me."

"Debra, give me a break," Terry muttered. "Don told me it was you."

He hung up.

"Oh. Hey!" Jenny dropped the phone to the bed.

"What happened?" Debra demanded.

"He knows," Jenny told her, frowning.

"Huh?"

"Terry knows it's you. Don told him."

Debra jumped to her feet angrily. "Don did *what?* That disgusting creep!"

Jenny picked up the phone to make sure she had turned it off. "The game's over, Deb."

"I don't *believe* Don! He — he's a filthy snitch," Debra fumed. "What right does he have to spoil some perfectly innocent fun?"

Jenny snickered. "It wasn't exactly innocent, was it?"

Debra glanced at the clock. "I've got to go." She shook her head angrily. "Now I have to run and hide every time I see Terry coming. I'm so embarrassed!"

"I warned you," Jenny replied playfully.

"Terry'll never let me live this down. Never!" Debra fretted, tossing her hair behind her shoulders. "And I'll bet he tells everybody."

She furiously kicked a pair of sneakers out of her way. "People will be laughing at me forever!" she wailed. "For the rest of my life!"

"Don't exaggerate," Jenny said softly. "After ten or twenty years, they'll forget. You'd better hurry, Deb. Mrs. Wagner warned you about being late tonight, remember?"

"Oh. Right." Debra checked her hair in the mirror, smoothed the front of her T-shirt, and hurriedly applied some clear lip gloss to her lips. "Why am I doing this?" she asked herself in the mirror. "Mark isn't coming tonight."

She dropped the lip gloss and started to the door. "What are you doing tonight?" she called back to Jenny.

"Not much," Jenny replied. "I'm going to take a long shower. Then maybe read a book."

"Lucky," Debra said. Then she disappeared out the door.

"Thanks for coming on time," Mrs. Wagner said, greeting Debra at the door. Debra followed her into the living room. "Now where did I put my briefcase?"

"It's right over there. On the chair," Debra told her, pointing.

"Oh. Of course." She scratched her thick, frizzy hair. "I don't know why I'm so nervous about this exam. I really know the material forwards and back. But it *does* count for half my grade."

"I get really nervous before tests, too," Debra said.

"What grade are you going to be in?" Mrs. Wagner asked. Then, without waiting for an answer, she said, "Peter's been a little fussy today. I think he may be teething. So he may wake up tonight."

"I can't imagine Peter being fussy," Debra said.

Mrs. Wagner picked up her briefcase, then put it down. She slapped her forehead. "I almost forgot my notes. I left them on my desk."

She fluttered out of the room, was gone for a few seconds, then returned carrying a sheath of papers in her hand.

"All babies are fussy when they're teething. Even Peter," she said, struggling to stuff the stack of notes into her briefcase. "If he cries really hard and you can't get him to stop, you can rub a little rum on his gums."

"Okay," Debra said. "He'll like that."

A few seconds later, Mrs. Wagner was out the door. Debra stood in the middle of the living room and listened to her car start up, then back down the drive.

Debra suddenly felt uncomfortable. The room, with all its figurines and photos and

knickknacks, seemed smaller and more cluttered than usual. She took a deep breath. The
air was so stuffy.

It was so . . . quiet.

Hope I'm not getting claustrophobic, Debra
thought. Maybe I'd better get out of this living
room.

She made her way silently up the stairs and
tiptoed into Peter's room. He was sleeping on
his stomach, snoring gently. An angel, as
usual.

Feeling a little better, Debra padded down
the stairs.

Why am I so out of sorts tonight? she
wondered.

Is it because Mark isn't coming?

She realized it was the first time she'd been
all alone in Mrs. Wagner's house for an entire
evening.

Maybe that's why the place seemed so much
quieter, so much stuffier, the cluttered living
room so much stranger.

Feeling a sudden tingle of fear, Debra decided to make sure the doors were locked. She
checked the front door, then made her way
quickly back to the kitchen.

To her surprise, the kitchen door was wide
open.

"Weird," she said aloud.

Mrs. Wagner always kept it closed.

She stopped in the center of the room, suddenly filled with fear. Had someone come into the house through the kitchen door?

She turned and glanced quickly around the large kitchen.

No one there.

Debra, stop spooking yourself, she scolded.

She moved quickly to the door, slammed it shut, and turned the lock.

She stared out into the dark backyard for a moment. No one there, either.

You're okay, Debra. There's no one else here, she assured herself. You're just a little edgy tonight. You're probably still upset about Don squealing to Terry that you were his "secret admirer."

Yes, that's it, she decided. I'm still upset about that. That's all.

She removed a can of Coke from the refrigerator, popped the top open, and took a few sips.

I wonder if Mark is still home, she thought, eyeing the wall phone. "Mark will cheer me up," she said aloud. Her voice sounded tiny, almost choked. She cleared her throat and punched Mark's number.

She let the phone ring eight times. No one picked it up.

Disappointed, she replaced the receiver. She needed to talk to someone. It would help kill the time. And it would help her get rid of that uncomfortable feeling that something was wrong tonight, something was strange.

Besides, weren't baby-sitters *supposed* to spend the whole night talking on the phone?

Should I call Jenny? she asked herself.

Should I call Terry?

No. No way. I'll probably never speak to Terry again. I'd be too embarrassed.

I'll call Jenny, she decided.

But just as she reached for the receiver, the phone rang.

"Oh!" she jumped back, startled.

Maybe it's Mark.

She grabbed the receiver. "Hello?"

*"Hi, Babes."* A low, whispered voice.

"Mark? Is that you? I can't hear you very well."

*"It's Mr. Hagen."*

"Huh? Who?!" Debra exclaimed.

The voice was dry, like the crackling of dead leaves, and sounded as if it were coming from far away. Debra had to struggle to hear the words. And when she heard them, she felt her entire body go cold with terror:

*"I'm alive. I'm back. Company's coming, Babes."*

# Chapter 12

"Did you tell Jenny about the call?" Mark asked.

Debra shook her head. "No. Of course not. She'd only freak."

Mark leaned forward and kissed her. She felt his arm slip around her shoulders. He pulled her close.

They kissed for a long time.

When it ended, she sat back on the car seat breathlessly and rolled down the window on the passenger side. Cool air filtered into the car. She closed her eyes and smiled. The air felt soothing on her hot face.

They were parked in Mark's blue Civic under the old abandoned railroad trestle near Miller Woods. It was a popular spot for Glenview students to park. But tonight, except for a two-door Buick Skylark on the other end of the long trestle, they were the only ones there.

Debra had described to Mark the frightening, whispered phone call of the night before. He had listened thoughtfully, tapping the steering wheel rhythmically with his thumbs, shaking his head in bewilderment.

"Who could it have been?" he asked. "Who would play such a dumb joke?"

"Jenny would probably say it wasn't a joke," Debra replied, letting the cool breeze flutter through her hair. "She would probably say it was Mr. Hagen, back from the grave."

Mark thought about it for a while. "But if it was Mr. Hagen, why would he call you and not Jenny?"

Debra laughed scornfully. "Because it *wasn't* Mr. Hagen, of course!" she cried. "Because it was someone playing a mean joke on *me!*"

"But — but — I don't get it." Mark tapped his fingers nervously on the steering wheel. "Maybe they made a mistake. Maybe they *thought* they were talking to Jenny."

Debra shook her head. "No way. Why would Jenny be baby-sitting at Mrs. Wagner's?" She rolled down the passenger window all the way. "Whoever was calling *had* to know it was me. Not Jenny."

"So it had to be someone who knows you, right?" Mark said, staring up at the dark, shadowy trestle through the windshield. "And someone who also knows what happened to Jenny back in Harrison."

"Yeah. That's right," Debra agreed softly. She pressed her face against the shoulder of his shirt.

"So who could it be?" Mark asked, slipping his arm around her shoulders again. "Who knows about that guy who tried to kill Jenny — Hagen?"

"Well . . ." Debra thought hard. "You do!"

Mark chuckled. "Yeah. Right. You told me the whole story."

"So it could have been you making the scary call," Debra said. She raised her head and smiled up at him.

He gazed down at her uncertainly. "You're kidding, right?"

She slapped his shoulder gently. "Of *course* I'm kidding. Don't be stupid. Now let's think. Who else knows?" She leaned forward to see his face. "Did you tell anyone?"

"Uh . . . well . . ." Even in the pale moonlight, she could see him blush. He avoided her eyes. "Yeah. I told a couple of guys," he confessed, muttering the words quickly.

"A couple of guys? Why?"

He shrugged, embarrassed. "We were hang-

ing out. At the Dairy Freez. You know. Just
talking and stuff. And I thought it was a pretty
weird story. So . . ."

"So you told it?"

"Yeah. Sorry, Deb. I didn't know — "

"Who was there?" she demanded. "Who did
you tell it to?"

"Well . . . Jon Hart was one," Mark said,
shifting uncomfortably in his seat. "And Davey
Marcus. That's all. Oh — and Terry, of course.
You know. Terry has a summer job at the Dairy
Freez. That's why we were there. Because he
can sneak us free cones."

Debra gasped. "Terry? Terry Donnelly?"

Mark nodded. "Yeah. You know. Terry." He
cast a suspicious glance at her. "What about
Terry?"

"Nothing," Debra answered quickly.

I can't tell Mark about my dumb calls to
Terry, Debra thought. He'll only get jealous.
It takes so little to make Mark jealous.

"Come on. What about Terry?" Mark demanded. "Why did you gasp like that when I
said Terry's name?"

"I didn't," Debra lied. "Why are you giving
me a hard time? I hardly know Terry."

Mark continued to stare at her, studying her
face.

Terry's the one, Debra thought.

It's clear to me now.

I can't tell Mark how I know. But Terry is definitely the one who made the creepy phone call.

He was paying me back for making a fool of him with my silly "secret admirer" calls.

Terry decided to make a secret call of his own. He heard Mark tell Jenny's terrifying story and decided he could use it to scare me.

Well, Terry doesn't know me very well, she thought angrily.

I don't scare so easy.

I'm going to visit Terry tomorrow at his job and let him know that I know what he did. And I'm going to tell him what a total creep I think he is.

"What are you thinking about, Deb?" Mark's voice broke into her angry thoughts.

"Nothing much. Really," she told him.

"You seem so far away," he complained.

"No. I'm right here," she said. She reached up, pulled his face down to hers, and kissed him.

The big blue-and-white sign in front of the Dairy Freez showed a smiling, red-haired boy, Dairy Freez Fred, holding up an enormous triple-scoop vanilla cone, a smear of white ice cream spread across his chin and cheeks.

"How gross," Debra said aloud, pulling her car into the lot and parking in the back. "And why can't they spell 'Freeze' right?"

She pushed open the glass door and angrily strode up to the counter. She saw Terry immediately. He was in back, filling one of the soft ice cream dispensers.

He was concentrating on not spilling the syrup, and didn't see her at first. Debra studied his uniform, frowning in disapproval. He was wearing a Dairy Freez Fred cap and a long white apron, stained with chocolate, also emblazoned with the grinning halfwit, Dairy Freez Fred.

Terry was short and thin. His curly blond hair, which he never seemed to brush, stuck out on all sides of his uniform cap. He looks like a little boy behind that enormous apron, Debra thought.

"Terry — hey!" she leaned over the counter to shout at him.

He looked up, startled to hear his name. Recognizing her, he smiled. "Hi, Debra."

He finished filling the machine, replaced the top, then strolled up to the counter, wiping his hands on a chocolate-stained rag.

"I can't give you any vanilla," he said, his green eyes peering into hers. "I just filled the machine. It takes a while to freeze."

"I don't want vanilla," Debra answered curtly.

"It's weird seeing you in person," he said, not seeming to notice her coldness. "Usually I just hear you whispering on the phone."

Debra could feel herself blushing. "That was just a joke," she sputtered.

"Ha-ha," he said sarcastically. He grinned. "I knew it was you all along."

"Liar," Debra said, frowning. "You did not."

"Sure, I did, Deb. I've always known you were hot for my bod."

"Shut up, Terry," Debra said, rolling her eyes. "I didn't come here to talk about *my* phone calls. I want to talk about *yours*."

"Huh? Mine?" His face filled with surprise.

"Did you call me two nights ago at Mrs. Wagner's house?" Debra demanded, staring at him hard. "Come on. The truth."

It was Terry's turn to blush. "Well . . . uh . . . yeah. I did call you," he confessed.

# Chapter 13

"Huh?" Debra gaped at Terry, feeling a surge of anger and surprise. "But — why? I mean — "

"I tried to call you, but you weren't there," Terry said. "I called too late. You'd already left. I got Mrs. Wagner instead."

Debra stared hard at Terry, letting his words sink in. "You mean you weren't the one — ?"

"Mrs. Wagner sounded really nice," Terry said. He suddenly noticed the stunned expression on Debra's face. "Hey, Debra, what's wrong? What did I do?"

"Nothing." She shook her head, trying to clear it. "I — uh — I got a scary call the other night," she explained. "Some creep. I thought it was you."

Terry snickered. "No. It was some other creep."

"I'm sorry," Debra said, backing away from the counter. She saw that the other two white-aproned workers were staring at them. "I'm sorry about the dumb phone calls I made to you." She could feel herself blushing.

"Hey, no problem," Terry muttered, blushing, too. "I kind of enjoyed them." He laughed, a nervous giggle.

He's so cute, Debra thought. Even in that stupid apron and cap.

She wondered if she and Terry would ever go out, ever be a couple. Suddenly, an idea popped into her mind. "You know, my cousin Jenny is staying with me for the summer," she told Terry, leaning over the counter so she could speak softly. "She's really great."

"Oh, yeah?" Terry pretended not to be too interested.

"Maybe the four of us could do something Friday night," she suggested. "You know. Mark and me. And you and Jenny. I think you'd like her."

Terry gazed at her skeptically. "Is this another joke, Debra? Is your cousin eight years old or something?"

"No. Actually she's forty-two," Debra joked.

They both laughed. Debra described Jenny to him. Terry lifted his cap and scratched his hair. His expression suddenly turned serious.

"Oh, wait. Is this the girl Mark was telling me about? The one who was a baby-sitter? The kid's father tried to kill her?"

Debra nodded solemnly. "Yeah. Poor thing. She's had a rough time. But she's really a terrific girl, Terry. I think you'd have a good time."

Terry carefully replaced his cap. He grinned at Debra. "I'll think about it," he said. Then he added dryly, "But with *you* involved, I know there's got to be a catch."

*The catch is that I'd rather be going out with you myself*, Debra thought, waving good-bye.

Friday night the four of them went to a very silly Chevy Chase movie at the tenplex at the mall. Terry giggled like a hyena throughout the entire movie. Jenny, sitting on the aisle, kept casting glances down the row at Debra, rolling her eyes as if to say, "What's *with* this guy?"

Oh, great, Debra thought unhappily. Jenny *hates* Terry. She's having a terrible time.

But when the movie ended, Jenny and Terry walked up the aisle arm in arm, giggling together.

Watching them, Debra felt a pang of jealousy.

Mark had a cold and kept wiping his nose on a shredded piece of tissue. He was in a sullen mood because of the cold and had barely said three words to Debra the entire night.

Terry, on the other hand, was in a jolly mood. He seemed excited to be with Jenny. As they walked to Mark's car, Terry talked enthusiastically about other Chevy Chase comedies he'd seen, telling some of the funniest parts, making Jenny and Debra both laugh giddily.

I've got to stop thinking about Terry, Debra scolded herself, sliding into the passenger seat next to Mark. I've got to stop being envious of Jenny.

Mark is a great guy. He's just in a crummy mood because of his cold. I like Mark a lot.

So why do I wish I were with Terry?

Why does this always happen to me when I'm going with a guy? Why do I immediately find a guy who seems a lot more fun and interesting?

Mark drove them across town to Page's, a small coffee shop that had bookshelves crammed with books on every wall. Jenny and Terry giggled together in the backseat of the car. Mark kept his eyes straight ahead on the road, sneezing and wiping his nose as he drove.

"Do you feel really lousy?" Debra asked, keeping as far from him as possible so as not to catch his cold. "Do you want to go home?"

"No, I'm fine," Mark insisted. "Really."

Squeezed into a small booth at the restaurant, the four of them talked about school and kids they knew. Jenny told about how she had almost ended up working in a doughnut store for the summer. She had them all laughing when she described her interview for the job and how she had seen the manager gobbling doughnuts the minute she left.

Terry started to tease Debra about the whispered phone calls she had made to him.

Debra caught the shocked expression on Mark's face and cut Terry off immediately. Terry blushed, realizing what he'd done.

"What calls?" Mark asked Terry.

"Uh . . . calls?" Terry asked, playing dumb.

"You just said something about Debra calling you," Mark insisted, turning his gaze on Debra.

"I just called him about Jenny," Debra replied, thinking quickly. "You know. To see if he wanted to go out tonight."

"Yeah. That's right," Terry added quickly, not very convincingly.

But Mark appeared to accept the explanation. He settled back in the booth and sipped his milk shake thoughtfully.

That was a close one, Debra thought, glancing at Jenny. Jenny and Terry were laughing together about something.

Serves me right, Debra thought. I deserve to get caught.

Why did I make those calls to Terry? Even Jenny thought I was weird for doing it.

She sighed to herself.

I guess I have a bigger crush on Terry than I'm willing to admit.

Forcing away those thoughts, she squeezed Mark's arm, then took another few bites of her hamburger.

"Good night, guys," Jenny said, pushing open the back door of the car. "See you, Terry." She flashed him a warm smile, then climbed out.

"I'll call you, Jenny," Terry said, sliding across the seat and climbing out of the car after her. "Sometime this week, okay?"

Debra gave Mark a quick good-night kiss on the cheek. "Feel better," she told him. Then she joined Jenny and Terry in the driveway.

They all said good night again. Debra wondered if Terry was going to kiss Jenny good night.

She found herself feeling relieved when he didn't. He climbed into the passenger seat beside Mark. He slammed the door and waved through the window to Jenny.

Jenny and Debra watched the car back down the drive and pull away. Then they turned and began to make their way to Debra's house.

It was a clear, warm night, sultry for June. A pale, half moon hung just over the sloping rooftop, surrounded by shimmering stars.

"I like Terry," Jenny said happily. "He's funny."

"Yeah. He's great," Debra agreed. "I think he liked you, too. I mean, he said he'd call you and everything."

Their sneakers crunched on the gravel drive.

Crickets suddenly started to chirp all around them, a shrill siren.

"Thanks," Jenny said, squeezing Debra's elbow. "Thanks for everything."

Debra started to reply, but stopped.

Following Debra's gaze, Jenny stopped, too, and uttered a low cry of surprise.

Something was lying in the low shrub beside the front stoop.

Something pale and pink.

"What on earth?!" Debra exclaimed. She started to move toward it. But Jenny pulled her back.

"What is it?" Debra whispered.

"An animal," Jenny replied, holding onto her cousin. "No. It's — "

They took a step closer. Then another.

In the pale light, they could see a small, round head. Arms and legs, sprawled over the shrub.

"It — it's not moving," Debra declared. "I think it's — "

"Ohh." Jenny let out a terrified moan. "Debra — it's a baby!"

# Chapter 14

Jenny uttered another low moan and sank to her knees on the gravel driveway.

Her eyes locked in horror on the unmoving pink figure. Debra raised her hands to her face and took a step back. Her entire body convulsed in a shudder of terror.

It's Peter, she thought.

"Maybe — it's alive," Jenny choked out.

Taking a deep breath and holding it, Debra ignored her pounding heart and made her way to the front stoop.

It's Peter, she thought. Peter.

I know it's Peter.

How did he get here? Who *put* him here?

She gasped as she came nearer.

And picked it up in one hand.

"Jenny — " she called, her voice trembling. "Look! It's a doll! It's not a baby. It's a doll!"

As Debra held up the naked, pink doll, a

strange laugh escaped her lips, joy and fear
and relief and horror all mixed together.

"Huh?" Jenny climbed unsteadily to her feet.
She walked reluctantly toward Debra, as if not
quite believing her.

"It's a doll!" Debra declared, laughing the
strange laugh again.

"But how — ?" Jenny started. "I mean, who
put it there, Deb?" She stepped beside Debra
and took the doll from her hands.

And saw the small piece of paper dangling
on a ribbon around the doll's neck. "It — it's a
note," Jenny stammered, reaching for it with
a trembling hand.

Debra grabbed it first and pulled it off the
ribbon. She unfolded it and raised it close to
read it in the dim light.

"Ohh." She uttered a low gasp as the
scrawled words came into focus:

*"Hi, Babes. I'm back. See you real soon. Mr.
Hagen."*

"This can't be happening," Jenny wailed. "It
just can't!" She raked her hands back through
her dark hair.

Debra shook her head thoughtfully, but
didn't reply.

They had made cups of hot chocolate to calm
themselves and carried them up to Debra's

room. Jenny had kicked off her sneakers and dropped onto the edge of the bed. Debra slumped into the desk chair. She held the doll in her lap, rolling it over in her hands.

"Put it down. Please," Jenny pleaded. "I really can't stand to look at it." She shuddered.

"Take it easy, Jen," Debra said with concern. "It was just a dumb joke, after all."

"It's *not* a joke," Jenny insisted shrilly.

Debra obediently lowered the doll to the floor, pushing it under her chair, out of sight. She took a sip of hot chocolate, cradling the white mug in her lap.

"He's back," Jenny said, her voice a whisper. "This time, he's really back."

Debra stared intently at her cousin. "You don't really believe that, do you?"

Jenny, lost in thought, didn't reply.

"Jenny, listen to me," Debra pleaded. "Jenny?"

Jenny still didn't reply.

Debra stood up and, carrying her mug of hot chocolate, crossed the room and sat down beside Jenny on the edge of the bed. "Jenny?"

Jenny finally looked up. Debra saw that she had chewed her lower lip so hard, it was bleeding.

"He's back," Jenny whispered. "He's alive."

Debra shook her head. "It's a dumb joke, Jen. A really cruel, dumb joke."

"But who — ?" Jenny started. "Who would *do* this to me?"

Debra sighed. She took another sip of hot chocolate. It was too hot and burned her tongue, but it was helping to calm her. "I'm not sure it *was* for you," she told Jenny softly.

"Huh?" Jenny reacted with surprise.

"Someone might be doing this to *me*," Debra told her.

"I — I don't understand." Jenny slid back in the bed and rested her head against the headboard.

"I didn't want to tell you about this, but I guess I have to now," Debra said reluctantly. "Someone called me the other night. At Mrs. Wagner's. Someone whispering. A hoarse kind of whisper. He said he was Mr. Hagen. He said he was alive. He said — "

"I *knew* it!" Jenny cried, her face turning pale. "I knew he was alive. I knew he'd come back to — "

"Jenny, stop!" Debra reached out with both hands and grabbed Jenny's trembling shoulders. "Please. Listen to me."

"But why did Mr. Hagen call *you*?" Jenny demanded, lost once again in her own thoughts.

"Because it wasn't Mr. Hagen," Debra insisted, holding on firmly to her cousin's shoulders, trying desperately to get through to her. "It's some stupid creep, playing a stupid joke. It *has* to be. People don't come back from the dead."

Jenny locked her eyes on Debra's. "Don't they?" Her words were more a challenge than a question. "Don't they, Debra?"

"No," Debra insisted, releasing Jenny's shoulders and climbing to her feet. "Let's think. Let's think of who could be doing this. Who made the call? Who left the doll in the shrub with the note?"

"I don't know," Jenny said weakly, biting her bleeding lip.

Debra began to pace back and forth, holding the hot chocolate mug between her hands. "I have a confession to make," she said after a while, avoiding Jenny's eyes. "I hope you won't be mad."

"Confession?" Jenny seemed to be only half-listening.

"I told Mark about you. About what happened to you back in Harrison. The whole story."

"That's okay," Jenny replied softly.

Debra continued to avoid Jenny's gaze.

"Well, Mark told a few other kids. Terry and a couple of other guys."

Jenny didn't reply.

"But I really don't think Mark or Terry or the others would do anything like this," Debra said, thinking out loud. "I really don't."

"That's because it really is Mr. Hagen," Jenny said with a shiver.

"No," Debra insisted. "No way."

"I just don't understand why he called *you*," Jenny repeated, ignoring her cousin.

The curtains fluttered at the window. A gust of hot, wet air blew into the room.

"Let's think," Debra said, starting to pace again. "Who could it be? Who?" She stopped in the middle of her bedroom and turned to Jenny. "I just had a flash."

Jenny shifted her weight on the bed. "What?"

"Did someone follow you up here?" Debra asked, her eyes lighting up excitedly.

"Huh?"

"Did someone follow you? Did you give my address to anyone?" Debra demanded.

Jenny stared back at her, thinking hard. "Just Cal," she replied finally. "But he — "

"Cal?" Debra dropped down onto the bed at Jenny's feet.

"You know. My boyfriend back home," Jenny told her. "But Cal wouldn't do anything like that."

"Does he know the whole story?" Debra asked.

Jenny nodded. "Yes. He knows everything. But I'm telling you, Deb, he would never play a mean joke like this. He knows me too well. He knows how upset it would make me . . ." Her voice trailed off.

"You gave him my address?" Debra asked. "My phone number?"

"Yeah," Jenny said. "But Cal isn't up here. He was going to get a summer job back in Harrison. He was going to — "

"Call him," Debra demanded. She jumped up and hurried to the desk to get the cordless phone.

"Huh?" Jenny pulled herself to a sitting position.

"Call him right now," Debra insisted excitedly. "Let's prove that it isn't him. Let's cross him off the list." She pushed the phone into Jenny's lap.

"But, Deb — "

"Call him," Debra ordered, pointing to the phone. "We might just solve the mystery right now."

"No. It isn't Cal," Jenny said softly. But she

obediently picked up the phone and punched Cal's number.

The phone rang once. Twice.

"It isn't Cal. You'll see," Jenny said confidently, holding the phone tightly against her ear, listening to the steady, rhythmic ringing. "You'll see."

# Chapter 15

Cal's mother answered after the fourth ring. Her voice sounded hoarse, as if she'd been sleeping.

"Hi, Mrs. Barton," Jenny said nervously. "It's me. Jenny. Did I wake you?"

"Yeah. I guess," came the gruff reply.

"Oh. Sorry. I didn't realize how late it is. Can I speak to Cal?"

"No," Mrs. Barton said.

"Huh? Is he home?" Jenny asked, startled by the curt reply.

Cal's mother cleared her throat noisily. "He isn't here, Jenny," she said finally.

"You mean he's out on a date or something?" Jenny asked, puzzled.

"He ran away," Mrs. Barton said. "Last week. We had one of our fights. About the car. And you know how impulsive Cal can be."

"Yes, I know — " Jenny started.

"Well, he ran away and we haven't seen him for a week. His father and I are worried sick about him." She coughed. Then she asked anxiously, "Is Cal up there? Did he follow you up there?"

"Uh . . . I'm not sure. . . ." Jenny replied.

White sunlight poured down on the stable, capturing everything in its hot glow. The ground sparkled up at the shimmering silver sky. The horses bobbed their heads nervously, expectantly, shifting their weight, tossing their tails, seemingly eager to get moving.

Jenny saddled a tall palomino, standing in the shade made by the horse. The heat seemed to radiate up from the hard ground. The sun is draining all my energy, she thought, struggling to pull the straps tight.

I feel so heavy, even out of the sun.

So heavy and tired.

The horse tossed its head, the pale yellow mane glistening under the brilliant sunlight.

Jenny raised a hand to shield her eyes from the sun. She tugged at the reins, but the horse resisted.

She tugged harder.

Someone was waiting for the horse, waiting in the deep shadow by the side of the stable.

"Come on, girl!" Jenny tugged the reluctant horse away from the fence.

Sunlight danced off the tall grass that fringed the narrow path.

"Come on, girl. Someone's waiting. I know it's hot, but it's time to go to work."

The horse uttered a low whinny and followed her slowly toward the stable, its hooves thudding loudly on the hard ground.

A flock of dark birds swooped overhead, black V's against the white-silver sky.

Jenny felt the heat of the sun on her shoulders and the back of her neck. It's weighing me down, she thought.

I feel heavier than this horse.

"Come on, girl."

As the horse neared the stable, the waiting figure stepped out from the shadows. Moving quickly, he raised his sneakered foot to the stirrup and hoisted himself silently into the saddle.

The sun glowed brighter. Brighter still.

Jenny shielded her eyes with both hands.

The horse whinnied. The rider found the other stirrup, then righted himself, adjusting his weight on the horse's straight back.

"All set?" Jenny asked. "Feel comfortable?"

The rider didn't answer.

The ground shimmered white. Heat rose up from the dirt.

"Everything okay?" Jenny asked.

Still no reply.

She raised her eyes to the rider.

"Cal!" she cried.

He grinned down at her, his spiky blond hair gleaming like white fire in the blinding sunlight.

"Cal! What are you *doing* here?" Jenny demanded happily.

He didn't reply. Instead he leaned toward her and stretched out his hands.

"Cal — no!"

But he grabbed her hands and tugged hard.

"Cal — please!"

With surprising strength, he lifted her up onto the saddle in front of him.

"Cal, what are you *doing?*"

He took up the reins and the horse bolted forward. The sudden burst pushed Jenny back. She leaned against Cal, his arms around her, the reins tight in one hand.

The horse bounced beneath her. She could hear the hard thud of hooves on the trail.

"Cal — I have a job to do," Jenny cried. "I can't come with you. Cal?"

His arms felt so good around her shoulders. She leaned against his chest, feeling secure.

The trail led up to sloping hills, brown from the summer sun. Tall pines jutted up on both sides of them, whirring past in a blur, glistening golden in the white light.

"Cal — we have to go back!" Jenny cried, shouting over the steady *clop clop* of the big palomino's hooves.

She didn't want to go back. She wanted to stay secure in his arms, wrapped up by him, and ride forever through the trees.

The hot wind blew against her face, ruffled her dark hair behind her.

And then, suddenly, Cal pulled back hard on the reins.

Jenny felt the horse's body tense. She watched its head pull up.

Cal tugged harder.

The horse stopped abruptly, silently. The hot air swirled around Jenny.

"Cal, we can't stop here. We have to go back."

Leaning snugly against him, Jenny turned and smiled up at him.

The sun beamed down, blinding her at first.

But Cal's face slowly came into focus.

His dark eyes burned into hers, as hot as the sun. And as she stared, the dark pupils faded — until he stared back at her with eggshell-white eyes. Solid white.

No pupils. No pupils at all. The blank stare of the dead.

He grinned. And as he grinned, his skin began to peel away, chunks of pink skin sliding down like Silly Putty, then dropping onto his shoulders, falling to the ground — until Jenny stared in horror at a grinning, gray-boned skeleton.

"Nooooo!" Her scream echoed off the dry, brown hills.

His white eyes stared blankly at her.

"Let go!" She frantically struggled to pull away.

But his powerful arms circled around her. And as they tightened around her waist, she realized the flesh had fallen away from his arms, too.

He was only bone now.

A skeleton with the inhuman strength of the dead.

The bones encircled her, tightened around her, holding her, pressing her tight against the leering skeleton.

"*At last I've got you, Jenny!*" its voice, dry as the swirling dust on the path, cried triumphantly.

"*At last I am going to take you to the grave with me!*"

"No, Mr. Hagen!" Jenny shrieked, still struggling to free herself from the skeletal grip. "Mr. Hagen — please! Let me go!"

# Chapter 16

Debra glanced at the clock in the center of the cluttered mantelpiece. Eight thirty-five. "Mark, where are you?" she said aloud.

She started to pace back and forth, her arms crossed over her chest. But Mrs. Wagner's living room was too small and crowded for pacing. Debra stopped, afraid she might bump a table or shelf.

It was Monday night. Mrs. Wagner had hurried off to her class at the community college, late as usual. Debra was looking forward to seeing Mark.

The floors creaked under the worn carpet. Debra sat down on the arm of the couch.

Why am I so jumpy tonight? she wondered. Every sound startles me.

I wish Mark would hurry up and get here. I could really use some company tonight.

A scrabbling sound above her head made her

gasp. She gripped the couch arm and listened.

Probably a squirrel running across the roof.

That's all. Just a squirrel, she assured herself, forcing her heartbeat to slow to normal.

I'm getting as nervous as Jenny, she thought unhappily.

Was that Mark's car on the street?

She hurried to the living room window and pushed aside the curtains to see out.

No. Just a car passing.

She pulled the curtains back into place.

Poor Jenny, she thought. She's been having the worst nightmares ever since Friday night. Dreams about her boyfriend Cal and Mr. Hagen, the two of them all mixed together.

Yuck, Debra thought, tossing her blonde hair behind her shoulders.

Poor kid. She's really messed up over this Mr. Hagen thing.

She's just so terrified. She really thinks that horrible man is going to come back from the grave to get her.

I'd better call her later and see how she's doing.

Again Debra heard the scrabbling sound, like someone climbing around upstairs.

I'm kind of freaked about everything, too, she admitted to herself.

I mean, I'm the one who got the call last week.

What if some nut is after Jenny — and me, too?

No. Stop. Stop it right now, she scolded herself.

I'm not going to get all frightened because someone is playing a dumb joke.

But what *is* that sound upstairs?

Walking with determined strides, she crossed the living room to the stairs and hurried up to investigate. Stopping at the landing, she peered down the long hall. It was empty and dark.

Taking a deep breath, she stepped into Peter's room and crept up to the side of the crib. The baby was sleeping fitfully, breathing in short gasps and thrashing his slender arms as if having a bad dream.

He looked so distressed, Debra was tempted to pick him up and soothe him. But she decided not to wake him. She checked to make sure he was dry, then tiptoed from the room.

Poor little guy, she thought, heading back downstairs. Is *everyone* having nightmares around here?

The clock on the mantel showed that it was nearly nine.

I'll give Mark a nightmare if he doesn't hurry

up and get here! Debra thought impatiently.

She peered out the living room window. The street was dark and empty.

Maybe Mark's cold got worse and he isn't coming, she thought. She decided to call his house. Taking one last glance out to the street, she turned and headed to the kitchen to use the phone.

Mark answered after the second ring. "Mark — you're home!" Debra exclaimed.

"Yeah," he replied.

"But I don't understand," Debra said. "It's Monday night and — "

"I'm not coming, Debra," Mark interrupted, his voice cold and hard. "Why don't you call Terry to come over there?"

"What?" Debra didn't understand. Why did Mark sound so angry?

"I heard about your little whispered phone calls to Terry," Mark explained.

"You did? Who — ?" Debra started, but stopped herself. "But, Mark — "

" 'Bye, Debra," Mark said coldly.

"Mark, those calls — they were just a joke," Debra said, her voice trembling.

"Everything's a joke," Mark said bitterly. " 'Bye."

He hung up.

"Oh, great!" Debra exclaimed aloud, staring

at the humming phone. "Mark — you're a jealous idiot!"

She slammed the phone down onto the wall and stormed around the room. "Ow!" Her knee bumped a kitchen stool.

"Aaaaagh!" Bending to rub her knee, Debra let out an angry, disgusted cry.

She cut it short, remembering the baby, and listened. She hadn't awakened him.

Who told Mark about the stupid phone calls? She wondered angrily. Was it Terry? Who else knew about them? No one.

Now she'd have to cry and grovel and beg Mark's forgiveness, and make a total fool of herself to get him back.

*If* she wanted him back.

She leaned her back against the kitchen counter and stared at the wall phone.

Yes. I want him back, she decided.

I don't want him to be angry at me.

She decided to call him right back and apologize. If she made up with him immediately, there might still be time for him to come over tonight.

As she reached for the phone, it rang.

"Oh!" Debra jumped back, startled.

It's Mark, she decided. He feels as bad as I do. He's sorry he was so awful to me. He realizes he was being stupid.

She let it ring a second time.

Should I accept his apology right away?

Yes.

She lifted the receiver to her ear. "Hi, Mark," she said, "I — "

"*Company's coming, Babes,*" a harsh voice whispered menacingly in her ear.

Debra was so startled, she nearly dropped the receiver.

"Who *is* this?" she demanded angrily.

Was it Mark? Was it Mark playing this awful joke on her? The thought stabbed her, stuck like a dark wound in her mind as she listened to the raspy whisper on the other end of the line:

"*It's Mr. Hagen, Debra. I'm alive. And I'm coming for you. Real soon.*"

The voice was so dry, so far away. As if it really were coming from somewhere beyond the grave.

"Who *is* this?" Debra repeated. Her knees suddenly felt weak, about to collapse. She grabbed the countertop with her free hand to support herself. "Mark — if this is you — "

"*I'll be there,*" the voice rasped. "*Wait for me, Debra. Wait for me. I've come from so far away to get you.*"

"NOOOO!" Debra shrieked.

She tried to slam the receiver back on its

holder, but missed. It fell from her hands, swinging wildly back and forth along the wall.

The whispered, raspy voice still echoing in her ears, she ran from the kitchen. Through the hall. Into the brightness of the cluttered living room.

She was in the living room doorway when the howling started.

High-pitched animal howling.

An inhuman wail, like the agonized cry of the living dead.

As she froze in fear, the inhuman howl grew louder.

It's so nearby, she realized, raising her trembling hands to her ears.

The hideous howl rose and fell like a ghoulish siren, a terrifying signal, a call from beyond the grave.

"It — it's inside the house," Debra said aloud.

# Chapter 17

Her heart pounding, the howls piercing through the room, Debra held onto the doorframe to steady herself.

It's here. In the house, she realized, gripped with fear.

It — it's upstairs.

She realized she was holding her breath. She let it out slowly and gasped in another one.

As another wail rang out, she suddenly recognized the sound.

It was Peter. Crying.

"He's never cried before," she said out loud. "No *wonder* I didn't recognize the sound!"

Still shaky, but starting to feel the fear drain from her, Debra hurried up the stairs. She found the baby on his back, his face knotted in anger as he cried, thrashing his arms and legs wildly.

"Peter, it's okay. It's okay. I'm here," she said softly, and lifted him carefully from the crib. "It's okay. It's okay."

He stopped crying the instant she picked him up. Opening his dark eyes, he stared up at her and whimpered softly, his face still red from his noisy protests.

"You scared me, fella," Debra said softly, rubbing the crown of his warm head gently till he stopped whimpering. "You really freaked me, you know?"

Peter stared up at her, silent now, his breathing normal.

"I thought you were that dead man, come to get me," Debra said, her voice a gentle whisper. She walked back and forth, holding the baby against her chest, soothing him. He felt so nice, so warm, he was helping to soothe her, too.

"You've got good pipes, Peter," she whispered. "You made quite a sound, fella."

He was drifting back to sleep. She continued walking back and forth, holding him close to her, whispering softly to him.

"First that awful phone call. Then your howls and yowls," she whispered. "You can't blame me for freaking, can you, Peter?"

He was sound asleep, gurgling softly, as she set him back down in his crib. She stood watching him for a few moments, feeling better, feeling calm, watching how peacefully he was sleeping.

But as she made her way back down the stairs, the ugly rasping of the voice over the phone returned to her.

Again she heard the ugly threats.

*"Company's coming, Babes."*

The ugly, menacing words repeated in Debra's ears, chasing away the feeling of calm she had felt upstairs in Peter's room.

And she remembered something else. She remembered something that tightened her throat and made her feel cold all over.

He had called her by name.

Mr. Hagen — or whoever it was — had called her Debra.

*"I've come from so far away to get you, Debra."*

He wasn't coming after Jenny. He was coming after her.

*"Company's coming, Babes. I'll be there real soon."*

But why?

Her head spinning with ugly, frightening thoughts, Debra took a few steps into the living room.

But she stopped short when she heard the scrape of heavy footsteps in the back hall.

# Chapter 18

Debra felt a cold shiver travel down her body. She took a hesitant step into the hallway.

"Mark, is that you?"

Had Mark changed his mind? Had he come to Mrs. Wagner's to apologize?

No.

Mark wouldn't come in through the back door. He wouldn't come in without knocking or ringing the bell.

"Who — who's there?" Debra called. Her frightened words came out in a choked whisper.

Mr. Hagen?

The dry, raspy voice on the phone had threatened to come for her. Soon.

"Who's there?" Debra called, a little louder.

No reply.

"Mrs. Wagner?" Debra's quivering voice revealed her fear.

Still no reply.

Then, another scraping footstep. A cough.

Keeping her back pressed against the wall, Debra inched her way to the kitchen. Over the rapid pounding of her heart, she could hear the raspy voice repeating its cold threats in her ear.

*"Company's coming, Babes. I'm alive and I'm coming for you."*

She stopped just outside the kitchen doorway, her legs trembling. "Mrs. Wagner? Are you home?"

Silence.

A rectangle of yellow light shone into the hallway from the kitchen. Suddenly, as Debra stared in terror, a large shadow moved into the light.

Swallowing hard, her throat as dry as cotton, Debra took a step into the kitchen. "Maggie!" she cried.

The large woman, wearing a bright fuchsia housedress over black leggings, had her back to Debra. She was leaning into a pantry cupboard, moving food cans around.

She turned slowly at the sound of Debra's voice, holding onto the wall with one hand for support.

"Maggie — what are you doing here?"

Debra demanded shrilly, her heart still pounding hard.

Maggie pushed herself away from the cupboard and took a few unsteady, shuffling steps toward Debra, a look of annoyance on her bright red face.

She's been drinking, Debra realized. She's drunk.

"Who are you?" Maggie asked, squinting one eye at Debra.

"I — I'm the baby-sitter," Debra stammered, keeping her distance.

"No. *I'm* the baby-sitter," Maggie insisted, slurring the words together, squinting angrily across the room at Debra. "I'm the baby-sitter."

"Maggie, what do you want?" Debra asked sternly.

"I on'y came for what's mine," the woman replied, tottering to one side.

Debra gasped, afraid Maggie was going to fall over. But the woman caught herself and straightened up, blinking hard as if trying to see Debra clearly.

"You have to leave," Debra insisted, trying to keep her voice steady. "Mrs. Wagner isn't here."

"I on'y came for what is owed me," Maggie repeated. "I'm the baby-sitter, see."

"You'll have to come back when Mrs. Wagner is here," Debra told her. Taking long, hurried strides, she made her way past the tottering woman and pulled open the back door. "Good night, Maggie. You have to leave now."

"I have a key," Maggie said, turning slowly. "I'm the baby-sitter." She took a shuffling step toward the door.

"Good night," Debra said, holding the screen door open for her.

"I'll come back." Maggie stopped a few inches in front of Debra, forcing Debra to step back. Maggie was breathing hard through her open mouth. Her breath smelled sour from a cheap wine.

"Good night," Debra repeated.

*Please, please, go away!* she pleaded silently.

"I'll come back," Maggie said, teetering toward the door. "I'll come back for what's mine."

Then she made her way slowly out the door.

Debra immediately closed the kitchen door, turning the lock. She stood with her back pressed against the wall, waiting for her heartbeat to slow.

"What a creepy woman!" she declared out loud. "Why does she keep coming here? Just to frighten me?"

The baby started to cry again. Debra hurried upstairs to take care of him.

What a night, she thought unhappily.

A short while later, Mrs. Wagner returned. Debra decided to tell her about Maggie's visit. "She was terribly drunk," Debra said, concluding her story. "She left when I asked her to. But she said she'd come back. This was her second visit. I didn't tell you about the first time."

Mrs. Wagner listened to Debra's story in open-mouthed disbelief. "I told Maggie *never* to come back," she said, shaking her head. "I had to fire her. She was a thief, and she drank all the time. She loved Peter. But I couldn't trust her around him. She was just too irresponsible."

"Well, she still has a key," Debra said. "She scared me to death. When I heard someone in the kitchen, I thought . . ." Her voice trailed off.

"I'll have the locks changed tomorrow," Mrs. Wagner said, frowning. She raised her eyes to Debra. "I don't think Maggie's dangerous, but I don't know for sure. I heard that she had to move out of her house."

"She's homeless?" Debra asked.

Mrs. Wagner nodded. "Yes. That's what I heard. She's living on the streets. Poor woman." She *tsk-tsked*, then kicked her sandals off and rubbed her feet. "It's getting late. I'll see you Wednesday night. I hope Maggie didn't frighten you too much."

"No. I was okay," Debra lied.

An hour later, Debra was lying in bed, staring up at the shifting shadows on her bedroom ceiling, unable to fall asleep. She had been thinking angry thoughts about Mark. He wasn't there when I needed him, she thought. He let me down.

But then she realized that she had let him down, too.

Maybe I'll call Mark tomorrow, she thought. Maybe I'll apologize for those dumb calls to Terry.

Or should I wait for Mark to call me? After all, the calls were just a joke.

She thought about Terry, how cute he looked in his Dairy Freez outfit.

Maybe the calls weren't a joke, Debra told herself.

I'll never get to sleep if I don't stop thinking about all this.

But she couldn't turn off her mind, couldn't stop the swirling images of all that had happened tonight.

Turning onto her side, she found herself

thinking about Maggie. Poor, drunk Maggie, squinting at her under the bright kitchen lights.

Debra wondered what it would be like not to have a home, not to have a place to sleep in, to have to wander from place to place.

Her thoughts turned to Mr. Hagen, to the frightening, whispered phone call.

She was hearing his dry, throaty voice for the hundredth time, replaying his ugly threats in her mind — when she heard the shrill scream of terror.

Debra pulled herself up.

The scream was coming from the next room.

Jenny!

# Chapter 19

"Jenny — what happened? Are you okay?" Debra clicked on the light as she burst into Jenny's room.

Jenny sat up groggily in bed and blinked at Debra.

"Jenny — what *is* it?" Debra demanded, her panic revealed in her trembling voice.

"Another nightmare," Jenny said, her throat still clogged with sleep.

Debra let out a long sigh of relief. Then she rushed forward to give her cousin a comforting hug. "Was it the same nightmare?" she asked softly.

Jenny nodded.

"Such a horrible scream," Debra said with a shudder. "I thought — "

"It's a horrible nightmare," Jenny interrupted. "This time, Cal and I were in the car, driving somewhere at night. And Cal's face changed. His skin dropped off in sickening chunks. And beneath his face was Mr. Hagen's. And — "

"What's wrong? What's happening?" Debra's father demanded. Debra's parents burst into the room in their nightshirts, their expressions frightened. "We heard a shriek."

"Jenny had another nightmare," Debra told them.

"I — I'm sorry," Jenny said, embarrassed. "I can't help it. I — "

Mrs. Jeffers *tsk-tsk*ed. "You gave us a scare," Debra's father said, shaking his head.

"I'm okay. Really," Jenny assured them.

"Do you want some hot chocolate?" Mrs. Jeffers asked, squeezing Jenny's hand. "A cup of tea, maybe? Or something cold? I could run downstairs and get you something."

"No. Please. I'm fine now," Jenny insisted.

After her parents had gone back to their room, Debra sat down on the edge of Jenny's bed. "Speaking of nightmares," she began reluctantly, "I got another phone call tonight. At Mrs. Wagner's."

Jenny's eyes grew wide with fear. Her fingers tightened around the edge of her blanket. "From Mr. Hagen?"

"From someone *pretending* to be Mr. Hagen," Debra corrected her.

"No!" Jenny cried heatedly. "It *is* him. It's him! I know it!"

"Jenny, calm down — *please*!" Debra exclaimed, jumping to her feet. "It isn't Mr. Hagen. It *can't* be. It's someone playing a really cruel joke. Mr. Hagen is dead. He's dead!"

Jenny raised her eyes to Debra, her face pale with fear. "Debra," she said in a whisper, "how do you know for sure?"

The stable was busy the next afternoon. Jenny found it hard to concentrate. She kept thinking about Cal, wondering where he was, wondering if he planned to follow her upstate.

Two day camps arrived at the same time with noisy, excited kids, eager to get up on horses.

Heavy, dark clouds rolled over the sun, casting the stable grounds in an eerie, yellow-gray light. The gusting wind carried drops of rain, an omen of the approaching storm.

Are you coming here, Cal? Jenny wondered, as she tightened the saddle of a patient brown mare. Are you coming to see me?

"Is it ready? Can I climb up?" a redheaded boy in a faded Simpsons T-shirt asked, stirring Jenny from her thoughts.

"Yeah. You're all set," Jenny told him. The

boy lifted his foot into the stirrup. Jenny gave him a boost onto the saddle.

She handed the reins to him and started to guide the horse toward his camp companions. He held the reins uncertainly in one hand, holding onto the saddle horn for dear life with his other hand.

He called something down to Jenny, but she was thinking about her nightmare of the night before, Cal once again turning into Mr. Hagen, and didn't hear him.

Where *are* you, Cal? The question kept repeating in her mind.

*"Hey!"* An angry cry broke into her thoughts. Jenny gazed around the crowded stable.

"Jenny — whoa!"

It took her a while to realize that Gary was calling to her. He was standing beside the redheaded boy on the brown mare, glaring at her angrily.

Seeing his angry expression, Jenny jogged over to him. "Gary, what's wrong?"

"Look." He made a disgusted face and pointed to the right stirrup. Jenny saw immediately that it hung down too far.

"How's this boy supposed to get his foot in the stirrup?" Gary demanded.

"Sorry," Jenny muttered. "I meant to tighten it."

"You sent him off with only one foot in the stirrup," Gary said, turning away from her to tighten it. "He could've fallen. What were you thinking of, Jenny?"

"Uh . . . nothing," Jenny replied, feeling her face grow red.

"There you go, guy," Gary told the boy, fitting his sneakered foot into the stirrup. "How does that feel?"

"Good," the boy said, still holding tightly to the saddle horn.

"Push hard with both feet," Gary said, examining the rest of the saddle straps. After making sure everything was secure, he led the boy over to his group.

Jenny headed to the barn to lead out another horse. She was halfway there when she realized she was being followed. "Oh. Gary. Sorry about that," she said.

He put a hand on her shoulder. "You okay?"

She nodded. "I just wasn't thinking."

"I didn't mean to yell," he said, studying her face. "It's just that . . . well, that was a pretty serious mistake."

"I know." Jenny could feel herself blushing again. She had a sudden urge to tell Gary everything — to tell him she'd been having these horrible nightmares about a dead man who was coming for her.

But instead she said, "I'll concentrate harder. I'm a little out of it today, I guess."

He nodded sympathetically, his eyes locked on hers. "Well, you're all finished for now. Everyone's saddled up. I'm going to lead them out on the trail. Why don't you take a short break?"

"Thanks," she replied gratefully. "And I'm really sorry. About messing up."

He turned and made his way quickly to his horse. She watched him lift himself into the saddle, and trot over to the waiting riders.

Then she raised her eyes to the sky. The dark storm clouds hung low over the hills, moving quickly like a gray-black blanket being pulled over the sky. From somewhere far in the distance, Jenny could hear the insistent rumble of thunder.

I hope Gary gets them all back before the rain starts, she thought.

A horse whinnied shrilly behind her.

"It's okay. It's just thunder," she told it.

Her nightmare flashed through her mind again. Had it been raining in the dream?

She shook her head as if trying to shake the dream from her thoughts. She strode over to the nervous, black stallion and stroked its mane.

She thought of Cal.

*Don't think about Cal*, she scolded herself.

The horse nodded its head, as if agreeing with her.

Thunderclap. That was the stallion's name.

Stroking the animal's neck, thinking about its name, Jenny had a sudden impulse.

Thunderclap was saddled.

What if I climb on and ride off? Jenny thought.

Gary told me to take a break. Clear my mind.

What if I ride off, gallop away? Into the storm.

Thunderclap is a perfect name for a horse to ride through the rain.

Jenny untethered the tall stallion from the fence railing. She realized her heart had begun to pound. She felt a surge of excitement as she lifted herself into the saddle.

Uttering a low whinny, Thunderclap backed away from the fence, eager to get moving.

Jenny adjusted her weight in the saddle, tightening the reins in her hands.

I used to be a good rider, she thought.

I used to go riding at the Harrison stables often.

But then I stopped.

I stopped doing everything I loved to do.

Well . . . today I'm going to *ride*.

"We're going to ride faster than the rain, aren't we, Thunderclap?" she called down excitedly to the horse. "Between the raindrops!" she exclaimed. "Through the thunder!"

She guided the horse toward the trail, bouncing unsteadily in the saddle, still getting used to the big horse's stride.

The horse began to trot as Jenny followed the trail toward the hills. As the trail narrowed and curved up through the tall pine woods, Jenny quickened the pace to a steady gallop.

It was dark as night in the woods. The wind whipped against her, heavy and wet.

It feels so good, Jenny thought happily. The cold, wet wind. The heavy, rhythmic bounce of the horse. The dark blur of trees whirring by.

The rain came, at first a gentle tapping against the hard ground. And then a steady drumroll. She felt it first in her hair, then on the shoulders of her T-shirt.

Jenny closed her eyes and allowed the horse to carry her, following the curving trail at a gallop.

The rain feels so good . . . so good, she thought.

So peaceful — so *cleansing*.

And then she heard the hoofbeats behind her.

At first she thought she was hearing thunder.

She opened her eyes and listened, not slowing her horse.

The rain pattered loudly against tree leaves.

The woods grew even darker.

The rumble drew closer. Not thunder.

Another horse.

Another horse on the trail, galloping hard.

Jenny gripped the reins tightly. She pushed her sneakered feet hard against the stirrups.

"Ride, Thunderclap! Faster!"

She listened as she rode, the dark woods alive with sound, cracks of thunder, the steady patter of the rain.

And the galloping horse behind her, coming closer.

Closer.

I know who it is, Jenny thought with surprising calm.

I know it's Mr. Hagen.

Riding hard.

I know it's Mr. Hagen.

Coming to collect me.

# Chapter 20

Debra peered out the kitchen window at the rain. A bright white flash of lightning illuminated the puddled backyard. In the split second of brightness, Debra saw water sliding off the sloping garage roof, cascading to the ground like a waterfall.

As a roar of thunder followed the lightning, she took a step back from the window. She listened carefully, hoping the loud noise didn't wake up the baby.

When is it going to stop? she wondered. It's been raining hard since the afternoon.

She walked to the wall phone. Leaning against the counter, she picked up the receiver and called home. Her mother answered after the first ring.

"Oh, hi, Mom. It's me."

"Is everything okay?" her mother demanded. "Is the baby okay?"

Why did she always assume that something terrible had happened?

"Yes, Mom. Everything's fine."

"Was the street flooded?" Her mother never ran out of questions. "I heard on the news that the Jefferson Bridge is closed because of the rain."

"I don't go that way," Debra replied, allowing a little impatience to creep into her voice.

"Well, if this rain keeps up . . ." Mrs. Jeffers' voice trailed off.

"I called to talk with Jenny," Debra said, sliding a tall kitchen stool closer and climbing onto it. "Is she home yet?"

"No. Not yet." Mrs. Jeffers couldn't hide the worry in her voice.

"Weird," Debra said. "She should've been home hours ago. Where could she be in this storm?"

"Beats me," her mother replied. "Maybe she went somewhere after work with some friends or something."

"Friends?" Debra asked.

"Well, she mentioned she was getting friendly with the head wrangler there at the stable," Mrs. Jeffers said. Static cut through the line, making her voice sound far away. "Gary somebody, I think."

"But Jenny would phone if she was going to

go out," Debra said shrilly. She decided there was no point in worrying her mother. She quickly softened her tone and added, "I'm sure she's okay. Maybe she's waiting out the storm in the stable."

"Yes. Maybe," her mother replied. "I'll tell her to call as soon as she gets in, Deb."

Debra said good-bye and hung up the receiver. She slid off the tall stool and walked back to the window.

Another flash of lightning. The backyard was lit up, brighter than day. The wet grass glistened eerily, as if electrified.

And what was *that?*

Something moving behind the low cluster of rose bushes?

No. Debra stared into the darkness as thunder rumbled.

Just a shadow. Something blowing around back there.

There's no one back there. No one.

She turned away from the window with a shudder.

A loud *crack* made her jump.

"Who's there?"

No. Chill, Debra. Just chill, she scolded herself.

I'm getting as jumpy and nervous as Jenny, she thought unhappily.

There are going to be a lot of weird noises tonight, she warned herself. Tree branches falling. Trash cans being blown over by the wind. Shutters banging.

You've got to stay calm.

It wasn't easy.

For the first few weeks, this baby-sitting job had been easy. And fun. Especially since Mark sneaked over every time she stayed.

But ever since the frightening phone calls, the job wasn't fun anymore. The house had become creepy, frightening. Just *being* here was frightening.

And now Mark didn't come to help keep her company.

"Mark, where are you?" she said aloud, anger in her voice.

Impulsively, she picked up the phone and punched his number.

A sheet of bright lightning made the room seem to explode.

Listening to the phone ring at the other end, Debra's heart began to thud in her chest.

Why am I calling him? What am I going to say?

I guess I'll apologize. And ask him to come over.

I'll tell him I'm afraid. That I really need him here.

Mark's mother answered, sounding half-awake.

"Oh, I'm sorry. It's me. Debra. Did I wake you?"

Debra glanced up at the copper kitchen clock above the sink. Only eight-thirty.

"I must've dozed off in front of the tube," Mark's mother replied, clearing her throat. "I can't even remember what I was watching. Some Wall Street show on PBS, I think."

"Well, I'm really sorry," Debra repeated. "Is Mark there? I really need to talk to him."

A loud crackling on the line drowned out the reply.

"I — I can't hear you very well," Debra said, shouting over the interference on the line. "Is Mark there?"

"No. He went out," his mother said. "He isn't home."

He went out in this storm? Debra thought. Where would he go on a Monday night in the pouring rain?

"Did he say where he was going?" Debra asked. "I'd really like to reach him."

There was a pause as his mother tried to recall. "No. Sorry, Debra. He didn't tell me where he was going. Some rain, huh?"

"Yeah, sure is," Debra replied, unable to keep the disappointment from her voice.

"Should I tell Mark to call you?"

"Yes. Please. I'm at Mrs. Wagner's. He'll know. Thanks a lot. Sorry I woke you."

"Stay dry," Mark's mother said.

Debra hung up dejectedly.

She leaned against the kitchen stool, staring at the yellow-and-white wallpaper, not moving for a long moment. Then she pushed herself off, turned, and pulled a can of Coke from the refrigerator.

After two sips, she didn't want anymore. She set the can down by the sink.

Lightning flashed outside. She could hear it crack and decided it must be nearby.

Where is Mark? she asked herself.

Where could he have gone during the worst thunderstorm of the decade?

And then she had an unpleasant thought: Is he seeing someone else?

She took another sip from the Coke can. It tasted sour to her.

"Oh!" she cried as the lights flickered out.

The sudden darkness lasted only a few seconds. Then the kitchen light flashed back on and the refrigerator resumed its loud hum.

Please, *please*, don't let the electricity go out, Debra pleaded, gazing out the window into the darkness.

I couldn't *bear* it tonight if the electricity

went out and I was here, alone, in total darkness.

The phone rang loudly.

She glanced around, not recognizing the sound at first.

A second ring.

Is it Jenny? Mark?

Or is it . . .

Feeling a stab of fear, Debra's hand hesitated on the receiver.

Maybe I shouldn't answer it, she thought.

# Chapter 21

The phone rang for a fourth time.

Debra swallowed hard and lifted the receiver to her ear. "Hello?"

"Hello, Marty?"

"Huh?"

"Could I talk to Marty? It's Eddie."

"Sorry. There's no Marty here," Debra replied, relieved. "You have the wrong number."

"You sure?" Eddie asked.

Debra hung up the receiver. "Yeah. I'm sure," she said aloud.

Why couldn't it have been Mark or Jenny? she wondered.

Creaking sounds from the front hall made her stop and listen.

Footsteps?

Was that a door squeaking? Someone walking quietly in the hall?

No. Just storm clouds, she told herself, not entirely convinced.

Just the house groaning. That's all.

She realized she was holding her breath. Letting it out slowly, she started toward the kitchen window. Rain pounded against the window as if trying to break in.

She was in the center of the room when the phone rang again.

*This time it's Mr. Hagen.*

The frightening thought broke into her mind.

*This time it has to be him.*

She suddenly felt cold all over.

The lights flickered again, dimmed for a moment, then came back.

The phone seemed to grow louder as it rang.

And louder still, until it hurt Debra's ears.

*This time it's Mr. Hagen.*

Please, please — no!

She lifted the receiver to her ear with a trembling hand. "Hello?"

"Hi, Debra. It's me. Everything okay?" Mrs. Wagner asked.

"Yeah. Fine," Debra managed to choke out, her heart in her throat.

"Did the storm wake up Peter?" Debra could hear a lot of background noise. Mrs. Wagner must be calling from a pay phone, she realized.

"Peter's the best sleeper in the world," Debra said. "The storm hasn't bothered him a bit."

"Well, I'm going to be out a little later than usual," Mrs. Wagner said, shouting over the crowd noise. "Is that okay, Debra?"

"Yeah. Sure."

"I'm going to have coffee with my instructor. It shouldn't be too late. But, Debra, do me a favor?"

"What's that?"

"If I'm not home by eleven, wake up Peter and feed him, okay? There's a bottle of formula in the fridge. Just take it out, pull off the cap, and warm it up. You know how to do it, right?"

"No problem, Mrs. Wagner," Debra assured her.

"Thanks, Debra. See you later."

The line went dead.

Debra sighed. *I really don't want to be here tonight,* she thought. *I'd rather be home.*

*Oh well, at least I'll make some extra money.*

Carrying her Coke can, she made her way to the living room. Lightning flashed outside the large picture window. The burst of white light made all of the figurines and miniature soldiers seem to flicker to life.

Debra stopped in the doorway.

Everything in the cluttered room seemed to be moving, crawling over the tables and shelves, rolling and spinning in the flashes of white lightning.

This room is too creepy tonight, Debra decided. She removed the book she'd been reading from her backpack and quickly returned to the kitchen.

Sitting on a tall kitchen stool, resting her elbows on the kitchen counter, she concentrated on her book and tried to ignore the rumbling thunder, the hard patter of rain against the windows, and the frightening creaks and groans of the house.

At a few minutes before eleven, she looked up from her book. Formula time for Peter, she thought.

She removed the cold bottle from the refrigerator, pulled off the plastic cap, and put it in a pot of water on the stove to warm up.

I wonder how Peter will react to being awakened, she thought. Will he be cranky? Will he want his mom?

"Only one way to find out," she said aloud.

Her footsteps made the floorboards squeak as she made her way to the stairs. About to head up the stairs, she stopped — and gaped at the front door.

It was open a crack.

"Whoa!" Debra exclaimed. A cold shiver ran down her back.

I closed that door. I *know* I closed it.

One hand on the banister, she froze in place, staring hard at the door, as if waiting for it to reveal its secret.

Didn't I close it?

Didn't I push it shut and listen for it to click as I wiped my wet sneakers on the mat?

What's going *on* here?

A sudden thought eased her mind: Mrs. Wagner went out the front door to get to her car. She was in such a hurry, she probably forgot to pull the door shut.

Yes. That's the answer.

Debra eagerly convinced herself that she had solved the mystery. Feeling relieved, she pushed the door shut. Then she hurried upstairs to Peter's room.

She stopped in the doorway. The only light came from a nightlight down by the floor. It cast a triangle of dim amber light against the wall.

She stepped past the low changing table, an open box of Pampers in the corner. Past the dresser, which had several stuffed animals piled on its top.

"Peter? Time for a snack," Debra called softly.

She leaned over the crib and peered down anxiously.

"Peter?"

The crib was empty.

# Chapter 22

"Peter?"

At first, Debra refused to believe her eyes.

Peter *had* to be in the crib. He *had* to be there.

"Peter?"

Squeezing the top railing of the crib with both hands, she stared down at the smooth white sheet and the light blue blanket crumpled in the corner against the wall.

"Peter?"

Why weren't her eyes cooperating? Why wasn't she seeing the baby? He *had* to be there!

Debra's hands began to shake. As her terror grew, as she began to realize that she wasn't going to see the baby in his crib, the shaking spread, until her entire body was trembling. She grasped the crib railing to hold herself up.

"Noooooooooo!"

It took her a while to realize that the long

wail of horror was coming from her own throat.

"Where *is* he?" she cried in a choked whisper. "Where? Where?"

She felt sick. She swallowed hard, trying to fight off the wave of nausea that swept over her.

"Peter?"

Without realizing what she was doing, she leaned into the crib and began pulling up the bedclothes.

She tossed the blue blanket away. "Peter?"

She pulled up the sheet. Then she grabbed up the foam mat beneath it and heaved it frantically across the room.

*"Peter?"*

This *can't* be happening!

Where *is* he? Where is he hiding?

Rain pattered hard against the bedroom window. A roar of thunder seemed to shake the house.

Debra stumbled blindly toward the doorway and clicked on the ceiling light.

*Got to find him. Got to find him.*

"Where are you?" Again, she didn't realize she was screaming.

Her eyes desperately darted around the small room.

They stopped on the dark footprint on the rug in front of the crib.

A dark, *wet* footprint on the shaggy tan carpet.

"Ohhhh." Debra sank to her knees with a low moan.

*Someone was here. Someone took Peter.*

*Someone stole the baby.*

*Someone was in the house. Someone . . .*

She crawled across the rug and pressed her hand on the footprint.

Still wet.

A fresh footprint.

"Noooooo!"

She forced herself to stand up. Her body felt as if it weighed a thousand pounds. She could feel the blood throbbing hard at her temples.

"What do I do?" Her eyes still raced around the room, searching, searching the dressertop, the changing table, every inch of the floor — until they rested again on the wet footprint by the crib.

"The police!"

Another powerful wave of nausea made her close her eyes. She swallowed hard. She felt hot and cold at the same time.

When she opened her eyes, the room began to tilt and sway. She pressed her palm against the wall, propelled herself forward to the doorway.

Fighting off her dizziness, she stumbled out

to the hallway. "The police. I've got to call the police."

*Who did this? Who stole Peter?*

*Who broke into the house and took the baby?*

The horrifying questions whirred through her mind as, gripping the banister, she pulled herself down the stairs.

"Ohh!" She stopped two-thirds of the way down when she saw the boy in the front entry-way.

He stared up at her with cold blue eyes.

He wore a black demin jacket over blue denim jeans, all soaked from the rain.

Debra reeled back, holding on desperately to the banister. She gaped at his short, spiky blond hair, at the red scar that ran along the bottom of his chin.

She recognized him instantly from Jenny's description.

"You — you're Cal!" she stammered. "What have you done with the baby?"

# Chapter 23

Staring up at her, Cal shook his head, sending off a spray of water. He shivered. "I — I didn't mean to scare you," he said quietly.

"The baby! Where's the baby?" Debra demanded.

"Huh? I haven't seen a baby." He wiped his shoes on the mat. "I rang the doorbell several times. I thought maybe you couldn't hear me because of the rain and everything. So I came in. I'm totally soaked. I'm sorry if — "

"I don't understand!" Debra shrieked hysterically. "You don't have the baby?"

Cal's eyes narrowed on her. His expression revealed his confusion. "Baby? No. I — uh — Is Jenny here?"

"Jenny? No!" Debra screamed. She started warily down the remaining stairs. "I have to call the police!"

Cal raised his hands, surprised. "No! I'll go!

Don't call the police. Please. I'll go. I'm not a robber or anything. I was just looking for Jenny." He backed up to the door.

"*You don't understand!*" Debra screamed. "The baby is missing! Someone took the baby!"

"Huh?" Cal's eyes widened and his mouth dropped open as he realized why Debra was acting so panic-stricken. "Oh!" he uttered in alarm.

"Don't go!" Debra pleaded. "Stay here with me, okay? Help me."

"Yeah. Sure." Cal started to pull off his wet jacket, revealing a navy-blue T-shirt underneath.

As he tossed the jacket onto the banister, Debra hurried past him to the kitchen.

She lifted the phone receiver from the wall.

"Nine one one," she muttered to herself. "I'll call nine one one."

She held the receiver to her ear and started to push the numbers.

She stopped with a startled cry.

Silence.

The phone was dead.

# Chapter 24

"What's wrong? Did you reach the police? Are they coming?" Cal asked from the kitchen doorway.

"The phone — it's dead," Debra told him, still holding the receiver limply in her hand.

He stepped into the kitchen, his eyes on the pouring rain outside the window.

"Someone took the baby and cut the phone wires," Debra said weakly.

"The phone might be dead because of the storm," Cal said.

"*Who cares? The baby's missing!*" Debra shrieked. She let the phone receiver fall to the floor and covered her face with her hands.

"I'll run next door," Cal said softly. "Maybe their phone is working."

Debra lowered her hands. "You will?"

"Yeah." He stepped toward the kitchen

door. "Sit down, okay," he told her. "Try to get yourself together."

"How *can* I?" Debra cried.

Cal pulled open the kitchen door. The sound of the rain grew louder.

"Wait!" Debra cried. "I'm coming with you."

"What for?" Cal argued. "At least one of us should stay dry. Let *me* go."

"No!" Debra hurried to catch up with him. "No, please. I don't want to stay here alone. I really don't."

Cal shrugged and pushed open the screen door.

Ducking her head, Debra followed him into the rain. Cal began to run, and she ran right behind him, slipping in the soft mud and deep puddles.

*It was the crazy lady,* Debra thought as the dark outline of the neighbors' house loomed ahead of them, like a giant, hulking creature.

*It was Maggie. It had to be Maggie.*

*She said she was coming back for what was hers.*

*She's crazy. Crazy!*

*Maggie unlocked the front door, sneaked upstairs, and stole Peter.*

*And we'll never be able to find her because she's homeless.*

*She could have taken Peter anywhere!*

Debra's hair was soaked. Rainwater rolled down her forehead and into her eyes as she followed Cal onto the back stoop of the neighbors' house.

Peering in through the window on the back door, she could see that the kitchen was completely dark, except for a dim light over the stove.

Cal searched for a doorbell. Not finding one, he pounded hard on the door. "Anybody home?" he shouted over the rain.

He pounded again.

Debra peered into the dim kitchen.

Cal knocked one more time. "Anyone there? Anyone?" He turned to Debra, brushing water off his eyebrows. "No one here. Next house!"

Debra leaped off the stoop and began running alongside Cal across the swampy backyard.

*It wasn't Maggie. It was Mr. Hagen.*

The frightening thought burst forward from the back of her mind.

*He said he was coming. Mr. Hagen said he was coming soon.*

*Jenny tried to warn me that he was really back.*

Crazy thoughts swirled in Debra's head as she ran, swirled like the wind-blown rain that drenched her. She tried to force them from her mind, to concentrate on getting to a phone and getting help.

Cal pushed his way through an opening in the tall hedge that separated the yards, sending out a cold spray of rainwater. Debra followed him through the hedge.

Gasping for breath, her temples pounding painfully, her leg muscles aching with every step, she climbed beside him onto the back porch of the next house. Stumbling over a low stack of drenched firewood logs, she pressed both hands against the wall and caught her balance.

Cal was already knocking on the door.

After a few seconds, a startled-looking middle-aged couple in matching brown bathrobes peered hesitantly out at them from the kitchen.

"Please — let us in!" Debra screamed, motioning frantically to the door. "We need help! We need the phone!"

The couple hesitated for only a moment, then pulled open the kitchen door.

"Your phone!" Debra cried, water running down her face, her hair matted flat on her head. "We need to call the police!"

The woman pointed. With a desperate gasp, Debra lurched to the phone on the kitchen table and, blinking away rainwater, listened for a dial tone.

Yes!

Debra pushed 911.

"Police Emergency Services," a woman's calm voice answered after the first ring.

"Help me — *please!*" Debra cried. "*A dead man stole the baby! Please help! A dead man stole the baby!*"

# Chapter 25

"I don't understand! I don't understand this at all!" Anger mixed with fear in Mrs. Wagner's voice. She paced back and forth across her brightly lit living room, a wadded-up tissue clenched in one hand.

Suddenly she stopped pacing and burst out in loud sobs.

A young, grim-faced policeman moved quickly across the room to comfort her.

Debra, sitting tensely on the couch, buried her head in her hands.

What a nightmare, she thought. It's a nightmare come true.

And then, with some bitterness, she thought: But it's not *my* nightmare. It's Jenny's nightmare that has come true.

She uncovered her face and gazed around the room. Cal sat beside her, his clothes soaked through, his head bowed, lost in thought. Two policemen talked together quietly by the window. A third policeman continued to comfort Mrs. Wagner, urging her quietly to take a seat in the armchair across from Debra.

Upstairs, two or three other police officers were exploring Peter's room.

The police had arrived at Mrs. Wagner's house five minutes after Debra's frantic phone call. Mrs. Wagner had returned a few minutes later, confused and frightened by all the lights and police cars.

She had reacted angrily at first, accusing Debra of being irresponsible, of letting this happen. Then, frantic with worry, she had apologized. Now she was collapsing onto the armchair in tears, sobbing loudly.

And where is Jenny? Debra wondered, clasping her cold hands together in her lap. The police had ordered the phone line repaired immediately. A repair truck had arrived within five minutes and restored the line.

Debra had called home to tell her parents what had happened. Her father was on his way over to Mrs. Wagner's now. Her mother was waiting at home — because Jenny still hadn't returned.

"I just don't believe it," Cal muttered to himself at the end of the couch. He was tapping the couch arm nervously with his open palm.

He turned to Debra. "Where could Jenny be?"

Debra shrugged. "Maybe Mr. Hagen has her, too. Maybe he's got Jenny and the baby."

Cal started to say something, but one of the police officers, leaning over Debra from behind the couch, interrupted. "I'm not sure I'm clear on what you were telling me before, Debra," he said softly, brandishing a small notepad. "Your cousin was attacked by this guy Hagen, and Hagen died? And in the past few weeks, he's been calling you and threatening to come here?"

Debra nodded. "I know it sounds crazy. But Jenny always believed he would come back from the dead. And — "

The police officer frowned and held up his free hand to stop her. "Whoa. You're stressed out, that's all. You don't really believe this guy Hagen was calling, do you? It *has* to be a cruel joke somebody is playing."

Debra stared up at him for a long moment without replying. Then she said softly, "I don't know *what* to think."

Across from Debra, hunched in the armchair, Mrs. Wagner uttered a loud sob. "If it was Maggie," she started, her shoulders heaving up and down as she cried, "if it was Maggie, we'll never find her. Never."

"Please, ma'am," a police officer said soothingly. "We'll find your baby, wherever he is."

"But she's homeless!" Mrs. Wagner declared, her voice cracking. "Homeless! We'll never find her." She shook her head miserably, dabbing at her red eyes with the wadded-up tissue. "Why didn't I change the locks?" she muttered to herself.

The police officer with the small notepad crossed in front of the couch and lowered himself onto the arm, next to Debra. "Is there anything else you can tell us that you didn't think of before? Anything at all that you remember? Did you hear footsteps or strange sounds? Did you see anything unusual?"

Debra raised her eyes to him thoughtfully. "There were strange sounds all night," she told him, "because of the storm. The house was creaking. The rain kept beating against the windows really loud."

She glanced at Cal beside her on the other end of the couch. "It — it was so noisy, I didn't hear Cal come in," she revealed.

Cal looked up. He stopped tapping the couch arm with his hand. "The front door wasn't locked," he explained, for the second time. "I just opened it and walked in."

"But why wasn't it locked? Why?" Mrs. Wagner demanded angrily, glaring at Debra.

Debra took a deep breath and started to reply. But the phone rang, startling them all.

Debra, Cal, and Mrs. Wagner leapt to their feet at the same time and started to the kitchen to answer it.

"Is it — is it the kidnapper?" Mrs. Wagner cried, trembling all over.

"Debra, why don't *you* answer it?" the police officer requested, putting a firm arm around Mrs. Wagner's shoulders to steady her. "Is there an extension I could listen in on?" he demanded.

Mrs. Wagner shook her head. "No. Only the one phone."

Debra made her way to the kitchen. Her hand hesitated over the receiver for a moment. Then, swallowing hard, she lifted it to her ear. "Hello?"

The raspy, whispered voice at the other end was familiar. *"Is that you, Debra?"*

"Y-yes," Debra stammered. She held her hand over the mouthpiece and, her eyes wide with fright, whispered to the police officer, "It's him. It's Mr. Hagen."

The police officer scowled and stepped up beside Debra, bringing his ear close to the receiver to hear, too.

*"It's me, Debra,"* the voice rasped, dry as dead leaves. *"I got rid of Jenny —"*

"Huh? You *what*? What have you done to

Jenny? What have you done?" Debra shrieked.

"*I got rid of Jenny, and I have the baby,*" came the frightening, whispered reply. "*Now do you believe me, Babes? Now do you believe I'm really back?*"

# Chapter 26

Her face twisted in horror, Debra uttered a low moan.

The phone receiver fell from her hand.

The police officer swiped at it, grabbing the cord, and pulled the receiver to his ear. "Whoever you are, listen carefully," he said sternly. But then his expression changed. He slowly lowered the phone. "The creep hung up," he announced, disappointed.

"He — he said he got rid of Jenny," Debra managed to choke out. Her entire body was trembling. She grabbed the back of a kitchen stool to steady herself.

"But my baby — !" Mrs. Wagner cried. "My baby?"

"I heard Peter crying in the background," Debra told her.

"Oh, thank goodness!" Mrs. Wagner declared. "Thank goodness he's alive!"

"*What* did he say about Jenny?" Cal demanded, his face suddenly as pale as his white-blond hair.

"He said he got rid of her. That's all," Debra told him, lowering her eyes to the floor.

"What else? Did he say anything else?" the police officer demanded.

"Not really," Debra replied, shaking her head. "I heard the baby crying, and I heard — "

"Can you trace the call?" Mrs. Wagner interrupted. "How will we find my baby? How will we ever find him?"

Debra pushed herself away from the kitchen stool and turned to face the others. "I know where he is," she said, staring hard at the surprised police officer.

"Huh? What did you say?" the officer demanded.

"I know where he is," Debra repeated. "I can take you there."

# Chapter 27

Debra hunched down in the backseat of the police car, watching the windshield wipers swing back and forth. Rivulets of water poured down the sides of the windshield, reflected in the lights of oncoming cars.

Debra stared straight ahead, hypnotized by the rhythmic click and scrape of the blades through dotted patterns of water, as the car, its red light flashing, burst through the sheets of rain, spraying up tall waves on both sides.

I feel like I'm on a ship, she thought. A dark, dark ship, carrying us further and further out to sea.

She sat between Cal and Mrs. Wagner, all riding in silence, all staring straight ahead. Two police officers occupied the front seats, their eyes on the twin beams of yellow light that cut through the heavy rain. Another police car, Debra knew, followed right behind.

In the darkness, houses and yards disappeared. The car swayed in the driving wind, crashed over waves on the road, making it seem to Debra as if they truly were on rolling ocean waters.

"Nice night," one of the officers muttered over the low crackle of the police radio.

"Are we almost there?" Mrs. Wagner demanded in a hoarse, trembling voice.

The officers hadn't wanted her to come, but she refused to stay home.

Moving her eyes from the hypnotic sweep of the windshield wipers, Debra glanced at Cal. He sat with his hands clasped tensely in his lap, his eyes narrowed, his features taut with worry.

"Here's the turnoff," the officer in the passenger seat instructed his partner.

Debra was thrown against Cal as the car spun off the highway, sending up a wall of water. The car bumped hard, then, with a roar, began its climb up the narrow road.

"Almost there," the driver said quietly, his eyes narrowed onto the bouncing beam of the headlights.

"But how do we know my baby is there? How do we know?" Mrs. Wagner demanded, panic revealed in the shrill trembling of her voice.

"I know I'm right," Debra told her softly.

"When Mr. Hagen was talking, I know I heard a horse whinny in the background. They've got to be at the stable. They've just *got* to be there."

"But why?" Mrs. Wagner cried. "Why would he take my baby to a stable?"

The car slid and bounced over the narrow road as it climbed. A flash of lightning surrounded them in white light, illuminating for a split second the windswept trees and tall shrubs, bending and bowing on both sides of them.

"He said he got rid of Jenny," Debra said, choking out the words. "Jenny works at the stable. Mr. Hagen must have gone there to . . . get her."

"But — but this man is *dead!*" Mrs. Wagner cried.

The officer in the passenger seat turned back to her, raising one hand, gesturing for calm. "Please, Mrs. Wagner," he said softly but firmly, "we're almost there."

"No self-respecting dead man would come out on a night like this," his partner muttered dryly, without a trace of humor. He leaned forward over the wheel, his face nearly to the windshield, and stared hard into the swirling rain.

"The stable gate is open," the other officer

said, reaching for something at his feet. "Go right through." He pulled up a large flashlight from the floor.

In the bouncing beam from the headlights, Debra could see the outline of the barn up ahead, a dark shadow against the purple sky.

"Cut the lights," the officer instructed his partner.

Now they were in complete darkness.

Debra shuddered, suddenly feeling cold all over.

*Jenny, are you in there?* she wondered, feeling her throat tighten with dread. *Are you and the baby in that dark barn?*

*What has Mr. Hagen done to you?*

Cal uttered a long sigh, but didn't say anything.

Debra knew he must be as frightened as she was.

The car rolled over the wet, muddy ground, then slid to a stop. Both officers pushed open their doors as the car came to a stop. Without saying a word, they climbed quickly out.

Behind her, Debra could hear doors slamming on the other police car.

One of the officers leaned back into the car. "Don't come out. Stay there," he ordered. "I mean it. No matter what happens, stay in the car." He slammed the door shut.

A flash of lightning illuminated the police as, hunched against the rain, they began jogging toward the dark barn. Their flashlights threw powerful beams of white halogen light ahead of them on the muddy ground.

Debra struggled to follow their progress through the rain-drenched windshield, but the glass began to steam up. Now she could see only vague shadows and shapes behind bouncing dots of white light.

"I can't just sit here!" Mrs. Wagner cried suddenly. She grabbed at the door handle. "I have to see my baby!"

"Mrs. Wagner — no!" Debra shouted.

But the panic-stricken woman pushed open the door and leapt out of the car.

"Mrs. Wagner — !" Debra called helplessly after her, watching her run through the rain, slipping in the deep mud, heading after the police officers toward the barn.

Before she realized what she was doing, Debra had scrambled out the open door. She heard Cal calling to her as she began to run after Mrs. Wagner, but she kept going.

Rain pushed her back, so cold, so heavy. Sheets of windblown rain drenched her before she had taken three steps, matted her hair against her head, nearly blinded her.

A flash of lightning illuminated Mrs. Wagner

just ahead of her, running hard, leaning into the rain with her hands outstretched as if reaching for her baby.

Beyond her, Debra could see the scrambling policemen, spread out over the muddy field, close to the barn entrance, their bright lights played over the ground.

"Is anyone in there?" A police officer's voice through an electronic megaphone rose over the pounding of the rain, the rush of the swirling winds.

"Is anyone in there? This is the police."

The bright lights were all aimed together now at the open barn doorway.

The electronic megaphone hummed loudly, then squealed, then carried the officer's stern warning: "This is the police. We have the area surrounded."

As Debra approached, breathing hard, shielding her eyes with both hands, she could see pistols drawn, revealed in the unsteady beam from the powerful flashlights.

"Is anyone in there? We're coming in!" the officer's voice carried over the roar of the rain.

"My baby! Is he in there?" Mrs. Wagner cried.

Suddenly, a flurry of movement from the barn.

Panting loudly, Debra shielded her eyes, squinting to see.

It was a horse. A horse trotting fast out of the barn, into the glare of the flashlights.

Forgetting her fear, Debra stepped closer to see. Closer.

The horse trotted out toward them, its rider sitting tall despite the downpouring rain.

Closer Debra stepped, ignoring the rain now, ignoring the mud, ignoring the thudding of her heart, staring hard at the rider on the tall horse.

"Oh!" she cried out and grabbed Cal's arm when she saw the baby held tightly in the rider's arms.

"Peter! Peter!" Mrs. Wagner was shrieking.

*"I'm alive! I'm alive!"* the rider called down in the hoarse, raspy voice, the voice that had filled Debra with terror over the phone.

*"I'm alive, Babes! I'm back from the dead — and I'm alive!"*

With a loud gasp of terror and disbelief, Debra let go of Cal. She burst past the police officers, who were too startled to stop her, and threw herself onto the side of the horse.

"Hand down the baby!" Debra cried, reaching up her hands to the saddle. "Jenny — please — hand down the baby!"

# Chapter 28

In the harsh glare of the flashlights, Jenny's face appeared hard and angry. Struggling to keep the horse steady, she cradled the baby under one arm, pulling the reins tight with her other hand.

"Jenny — please!" Debra begged, reaching up to her. "Hand down the baby!"

Jenny's eyes narrowed in fury as she glared down at her cousin. *"I'm not Jenny!"* she rasped in the ugly, throaty voice. *"I'm Mr. Hagen, and I'm back!"*

"Jenny — please!" Debra pleaded.

*"You didn't believe me, but I'm here!"* Jenny cried. *"I'm here, and I've got my baby back! The baby-sitter killed my baby — but now I've got it back!"*

Poor Jenny, Debra thought.

Poor, poor Jenny.

"Please, give me the baby," Debra demanded again, reaching up both hands to her wild-eyed cousin.

The horse uttered a whinny of protest, bucking its head, shaking off rainwater.

Debra saw the police start to close in. She saw the glint of pistols in the bright light of the flashlights. She heard Mrs. Wagner sobbing somewhere behind her.

"Hand over the baby," the officer ordered, his voice blaring through the electronic megaphone.

Debra could feel the panic choking her as the officers moved forward in a circle. "Don't shoot her!" she screamed. "Don't shoot!"

*"I'm alive! I'm back from the grave! And I have my baby!"* Jenny screamed — and raised the baby high in the air, holding it in one palm. The baby thrashed its arms and legs wildly, wailing at the top of its lungs.

The officers moved forward, pistols poised.

"Don't shoot! Don't shoot!" Debra repeated.

And then she uttered a horrified scream and shut her eyes at the loud crack of gunfire.

# Chapter 29

Loud sobs bursting from her throat, Debra opened her eyes in time to see the horse rear up.

Jenny slid off the saddle, still holding the wailing baby high. She hit the ground hard and collapsed on her back in the mud.

A police officer grabbed the baby with both hands and brought him close to his chest. He stepped back to hand the baby to Mrs. Wagner.

Other officers, their guns still drawn, surrounded Jenny.

"You killed her!" Debra screamed. "You killed Jenny!"

She felt Cal's hand on her quivering shoulder. But she pulled away from him and plunged past the circle of dark-uniformed police.

"Jenny! Jenny! You killed Jenny!"

Debra dropped to her knees in the cold mud beside her fallen cousin.

Jenny gazed up at her, then sat up slowly. "I fell," she said, her expression bewildered.

"But — you're shot!" Debra cried, grabbing Jenny's arm with both hands.

A police officer gently pulled Debra's hand away. "It was a crack of lightning. Close by," he told her in a low voice. "We didn't shoot. Lightning made the horse rear up, and your cousin fell."

Crouching on her knees, Debra burst into tears, tears of relief. A few seconds later, she felt someone pulling her to her feet.

"It's going to be okay now. It's going to be okay," Cal whispered soothingly. He wrapped his arms around her, trying to comfort her.

Two police officers, their flashlights circling the ground ahead of them, were guiding Jenny to a squad car. She walked willingly, staring straight ahead. In the flickering, darting light, Debra saw her dazed expression.

"Poor Jenny," she muttered, leaning against Cal. "She's so mixed up. I — I can't believe she did all those things, made those horrible phone calls, left the doll in the bushes, tried to make me believe that — "

Cal held her tighter. "Mr. Hagen *was* alive," he said sadly. "In Jenny's mind. She kept him alive by thinking about him all the time. She —

she was so obsessed by him, he finally took over her mind completely."

"If only I'd realized," Debra said sadly, walking with Cal toward the waiting police car. "If only I'd known . . ."

"You can't blame yourself," Cal said, his arm still gently around her shoulders. "I spent a lot of time with her, too. I should've seen how troubled she was."

"Well, at least now Jenny will get the help she needs. She'll be okay," Debra said, wiping away the last of her tears with the back of her hand.

"And Mr. Hagen can go back where he belongs," Cal said. "Back to the grave forever."

A police officer held open the back door of a squad car for them. Debra started to climb in, but stopped.

She raised her face to the sky.

"This really is the end of the nightmare," she said, turning back to Cal.

Cal looked up and saw it, too.

A pale half moon peeked through the clouds.

The rain had stopped.

# THE BABY-SITTER IV

*This book is dedicated to Kristin Baker*

# Prologue

"I'm back, Jenny," Mr. Hagen growled. The grin didn't waver on his fleshless, decayed face. "I'm back, and I've come for you." His black, empty eye sockets stared at her.

"No!" Jenny Jeffers cried. Her breath caught in her throat, but she forced herself to scream out her anger. "No — you're dead! You've been dead for three years!"

She stared at the tall figure. Mr. Hagen. The man who hated baby-sitters. He was crazy. Totally crazy.

Jenny had been the Hagens' baby-sitter.

Until Mr. Hagen had tried to kill her.

But she had lived. And he had died.

For three years, the memory of the horror had followed Jenny. Haunted her. Until it had driven Jenny over the edge. Until it had taken away all reality. Until the real world had vanished behind a cloud of frightening fantasy.

It had been too much. Too much for a six-teen-year-old girl to bear. And so Jenny had retreated, retreated into a world of angry dreams.

A world without time. Without warmth. Without color.

A dark world of anger. And fear.

And now he was back.

Back from the grave.

Mr. Hagen's rotting body stood grinning at her. Threatening her again. "I'm back," he announced. His voice harsh and dry, like the scrape of dead leaves.

"I've come back for you, Jenny."

"No!" she screamed, feeling her anger burn into rage. Feeling all of her muscles tighten. Her chest about to burst.

"No! You're dead! You're dead!"

She raised the silvery metal baseball bat. It felt surprisingly light in her hands.

She leaped forward. Swung hard.

The bat made a satisfying *thud* as it caught him hard in the midsection.

His body bent in reaction. The big arms flayed out. The decaying head bobbed.

With a grunt of effort, Jenny pulled the bat back. Swung again. Harder this time.

The bat made a soft *thwock* as it smashed into his face. His body whipped around. The legs buckled. The arms swayed lifelessly at his sides.

"You're *dead*!" Jenny shrieked. "Dead! Dead! Dead!"

Another hard swing sent him spinning. Jenny uttered an angry cry. Sent the bat crashing into his back. Another hard blow to the shoulder. Another blow to the back of the skull.

"You're dead! You're *dead*!" she screamed with each swing.

Mr. Hagen bobbed and twisted. Helpless against her furious attack. His head tilted back. The stuffing fell from an open tear in his chest, scattering over the grass.

Again. Again.

Jenny continued to batter him, shouting out her anger, letting out all of her fury.


"Very good, Jenny."

Dr. Morton placed a calming hand on her shoulder. He had been taking care of Jenny since she had been admitted to the hospital a year ago.

Jenny let the bat fall from her hands. She struggled to catch her breath. Her entire body trembled. Beads of hot sweat ran down her face.

"Now you are really getting into it," Dr.

Morton said, bending to pick up the bat. His white lab coat fluttered in the breeze. "You are learning how to get those angry feelings out, aren't you?"

Still breathing hard, Jenny nodded. She raised her eyes to the battered dummy, swinging from the low tree branch. The painted grin on the pillow head was all lopsided now.

"I really did knock the stuffing out of it," she declared. Shreds of white foam rubber lay scattered over the ground.

Dr. Morton tapped the end of the bat against the dummy's torn chest. "I don't think this guy will bother you again." He flashed her a smile as he pushed his glasses up on his nose. "How do you feel, Jenny?"

"Much better," she replied quickly. She turned and started to follow him back into the hospital. "I think I hit a few home runs."

I *do* feel much better, Jenny told herself. The anger, the fear — the incredible fear — it's all gone.

I'm almost ready to leave this hospital and go home, she realized happily.

And I'm never going to be afraid again.

Never.

# Chapter 1

"BOO!" The hideous green face pressed up against Jenny's cheek.

Jenny groaned and rolled her eyes.

"Rick, give us a break!" Claire exclaimed. "That mask is totally gross."

"Totally," Rick repeated. He set the mask down on the display counter. Then he brushed his curly, black hair back into place. "Why do you think they sell Halloween masks in the summer?" he asked.

"Oh, I know," Rick declared, answering his own question. "For bank robbers to wear."

Jenny laughed.

Claire just stared back at him. She never got Rick's jokes. "How about some food?" she suggested. "I'm starving." She pointed to the Pizza Oven, the restaurant across the broad aisle.

Jenny followed her two friends out of the

store. The three of them had been making their way slowly through the mall, checking out different stores, laughing and joking around. Not buying anything. Just hanging out.

Hanging out.

Like normal people.

It meant so much to Jenny to be back with her two best friends. Hanging out. Kidding around.

Catching up.

She had been away from her normal life for an entire year. A whole year in the hospital. A whole year missing from her life.

Now it was summer again. A summer Jenny was determined to enjoy.

No anger. No fear. A fresh start.

Rick stopped at the restaurant window and pressed his nose against the glass, startling the kids at the table inside. Claire groaned and shoved him toward the door. "Grow up," she muttered. "You're such a baby."

"Goo goo," he replied. He sucked his thumb.

Claire didn't laugh.

"Give up," Jenny told Rick. "Claire is never going to laugh at your jokes."

"I don't call that a joke," Claire said dryly.

The two of them make such a weird couple, Jenny thought, stepping into the restaurant.

Claire is so serious, and Rick never stops goofing around.

But they've been serious about each other for nearly a year, Jenny realized.

While Jenny had been in the hospital, Claire had written to her every week. And most of her letters were about Rick and how much she cared about him.

Jenny watched Claire slide into the red vinyl booth. Claire was tall and thin, nearly a foot taller than Jenny. She had straight, brown hair, which she had streaked with blond this summer. She had it tied back into a long ponytail. She wore a pale blue tank top over white tennis shorts.

Rick piled in after her, bumping her with his shoulder, sliding until he squeezed her against the wall. "Move over! There's no room!" he cried. "Wow, are you getting fat!"

"Ha-ha," Claire replied. She elbowed him in the ribs, forcing him to edge away.

Rick pushed back his thick, black hair with one hand. He never brushed his hair, just shoved it back. He was a big teddy bear. Kind of good-looking, Jenny thought, with that broad forehead and those dark, playful eyes.

Jenny slid in across from them. She took a deep breath, inhaling the sweet aroma of cheese and tomato sauce. "The pizza in the hospital was terrible," she told them. "It was soft and doughy. And I think they used fake cheese."

"It comes from cardboard cows," Rick joked.

Jenny and Claire ignored him.

A young, blond waitress stepped up to the booth, adjusting the sleeves of her red-and-white-checked uniform. "What can I get you?"

"Do you have any fake cheese?" Rick asked.

The waitress narrowed her eyes at him. "I could check."

"Don't pay any attention to him," Claire told her. She ordered a large pepperoni pizza and a pitcher of Coke.

Jenny settled back against the seat. "Are you both working at the shoe store again this summer?" she asked. Rick's uncle owned a shoe store at the mall.

"No way!" Claire exclaimed, shaking her head. "Never again."

Rick bent down, pulled off his sneaker — a white Nike high-top — and placed it on the table. "You like it?" he asked Jenny. "I can get you a twenty percent discount."

"No thanks." Jenny laughed. "Guess you're back at the store, huh?"

Rick nodded. "Uncle Bill made me an offer I couldn't refuse. He named me assistant manager."

Claire rolled her eyes. "Rick's uncle has three salespeople. He made them all assistant managers."

"So what?" Rick cried. "I still get the assistant manager's discount."

The waitress returned with a pitcher of Coke and three glasses. She stared down at Rick's sneaker on the table.

"I'm going to drink from that," Rick told her.

The waitress didn't crack a smile. "We get a lot of funny people in here," she muttered. She set down the pitcher, turned, and strode away.

Rick blushed. Jenny and Claire laughed. Rick removed the sneaker from the table and bent to put it back on.

"The worst part about selling shoes is the lacing," Claire told Jenny, pouring the Coke into glasses. "You spend all day lacing sneakers, lacing sneakers, lacing sneakers. It takes forever. And then the customer is never happy. You laced it too loose. Too tight. Too high. Too low. Aaagggh!" She let out a cry, wrapped her hands around Rick's neck, and playfully pretended to strangle him.

"Hey — !" He pulled away from her. "Don't blame *me* if you don't have what it takes to be an assistant manager!"

Even Claire had to laugh at that.

"So where are you working this summer?" Jenny asked her.

Claire took a long sip of soda. "At the community pool."

"She's a drowning instructor!" Rick joked.

"I'm working at the food stand," Claire continued, ignoring him. "It's okay. I get to swim during my breaks. And I get to see a lot of kids from school."

Rick waved across the restaurant to some friends. "Back in a minute," he said. He slid out and made his way to their table. Jenny watched him slapping high fives and cracking jokes.

Claire's serious, brown eyes locked on Jenny. "And what are you doing this summer? Just hanging out?"

Jenny nodded. "Yeah. You know. Getting back to normal."

"How's your mom?" Claire asked.

"Really good," Jenny told her. "She got a new job, which she really likes."

"As a legal secretary?"

Jenny nodded. "Yeah. And she's been busy fixing up our new house."

"How do you like it?" Claire asked.

Jenny shrugged. "It's okay. Just kind of weird for me. You know. Getting out of the hospital and going home to a whole new neighborhood."

Jenny twirled the fork between her fingers. "Mom's really happy to have me home. Of course. And . . . guess what? She's seeing a guy."

Claire's mouth dropped open. "Your mom? That's great!" she exclaimed.

Since her divorce, Jenny's mother had been pretty lonely. Lonely and depressed.

When Jenny came home from the hospital, she knew immediately that something had changed. Her mother had darkened the gray in her hair. Her clothes were younger-looking. And she seemed so cheerful and energetic.

"Who is he?" Claire demanded. "Have you met him? Is he nice?"

Jenny snickered. "His name is Winston. Isn't that the pits?"

Claire narrowed her eyes at Jenny. "Is that his first name or his last?"

"His first," Jenny replied. "Everyone calls

him Win. I met him the other night. He seems really nice. He's very good-looking. Tanned. Blue eyes. Sort of a blond prince type. I think he's younger than she is."

"Wow," Claire murmured. "Lots of changes in your life, huh?"

Jenny sighed. "Yeah. Well . . . I've been away for a whole year, you know."

"I know," Claire replied, lowering her eyes. And then she added in a low voice, "You seem changed, too."

The comment caught Jenny by surprise. "Huh? What do you mean?"

Claire spun the Coke glass between her hands. "Better. You seem a lot better," she replied thoughtfully. "You seem stronger somehow, Jenny. More like your old self. Before . . . before . . ." Her voice trailed off.

"Before Mr. Hagen and all the horror?" Jenny finished the sentence for her friend. "Go ahead. You can say it, Claire. I'm not afraid anymore. You're right about me being changed. The year in the hospital changed me completely."

Jenny leaned across the table. She squeezed Claire's hands. "I'm not afraid anymore, Claire. I'm not afraid of anything now. I *am* much stronger. I *am* the old me."

Jenny was startled to see tears form in

Claire's eyes. "I'm glad," Claire said, wiping them away with her fingers. "I really am."

The pizza tasted delicious. The sound of normal, happy voices ringing through the crowded restaurant made Jenny feel even better.

She felt so wonderful being back with her friends, back in her real life.

Things are going to be great from now on, she promised herself. From now on . . .

But, then, as Rick dropped her off in front of her new house, as she waved good night to him and Claire, as she watched his little red Civic back down the driveway and disappear into the night, as she turned to the walk that led to her front door — Jenny saw a dark figure step out from the shadows at the side of the house.

# Chapter 2

She gasped. Felt a chill of fear.

*No!*

No! she told herself. I'm not afraid.

No more running from shadows.

She took a deep breath, then walked toward the figure. He stepped into the pale light from the porch.

"Cal!" Jenny cried. "What are you doing here?"

He hurried across the driveway to her. She threw her arms around him, hugged him close.

They kissed.

A whole year without any kisses, she thought, keeping her eyes open, wanting to see him, wanting to stare into those pale blue eyes of his.

A whole year without kisses. Is that why Cal and I have gotten so much closer? Is that why our relationship has become so intense?

She and Cal had been seeing each other before the horrible events of last summer. But she hadn't felt so deeply about him then.

She hugged him tighter. Took a deep breath. Kissed him again.

I'm so grateful for Cal, Jenny thought. He stayed with me. He didn't abandon me. He wrote to me. The letters we wrote to each other helped me so much, helped me to remember that I had a real life waiting for me back home.

Cal gave me a good reason to get out of the hospital. And stay out.

I'm going to stay healthy for you, Cal, Jenny promised silently, stroking the back of his white-blond hair. I'm going to stay brave for you, Cal.

When they finished the kiss, they both were breathless.

"Sorry," Cal whispered. "Sorry I didn't meet you guys at the mall."

"Where were you?" Jenny asked softly, holding his hand between hers.

"Had to work an extra shift," Cal told her with a sigh. The tiny gold stud in his ear caught the light from the porch. "One of the guys was sick. So you-know-who gets to stay and pump gas."

She let go of his hand and leaned against

him. His T-shirt smelled of gasoline. So did his hands. "At least you have a job this summer," she murmured.

"Yeah. I guess."

She pressed both hands against the front of his shirt. His chest felt so solid. "You won't have to work Saturday night — right?"

He nodded. "I already told Hansen. He gave me a hard time. Do you believe it? Like I haven't worked double shifts for the guy all week."

Cal shook his head. Jenny saw a flash of anger in his eyes. "Man, I hate that guy!" Cal exploded. "He thinks he's hot stuff because he owns one lousy gas station."

Jenny raised a hand to his shoulder to calm him. But Cal shook it away.

"He doesn't even *own* the station," he continued bitterly. "His brother-in-law owns it. But Hansen thinks he's king of the world. You should hear him yelling at me because I left the cash register open."

"Cal — please!" Jenny insisted quietly. She hated when Cal went into one of his rages. Normally, he was so quiet. But he had an angry side. Jenny never knew what might touch it off, make him explode with rage.

Cal always managed to get himself in control. But it frightened Jenny. It frightened her a lot. And it made her think there was a whole side of Cal — an angry, bitter side — she didn't know at all.

"We're going out Saturday night, and that's that!" Cal said heatedly. "And if Hansen tells me I have to work late, I — I'll just quit."

"No, you won't," Jenny replied quickly. "You won't quit," she scolded. "You need the money, and you know it."

Cal's dad had been laid off from the box factory where he was a foreman. The family was living on his mom's salary as assistant store manager at Wal-Mart.

"Stop talking so crazy and kiss me good night," Jenny instructed.

The kiss lasted a long time.

When it ended, Jenny pushed herself away from him with both hands. "See you," she murmured breathlessly. And ran into her house without glancing back.

Jenny's mother had gone to bed. The house was dark except for the front entry light.

Jenny made her way quickly up the stairs to her room. She clicked on the ceiling light and stepped inside.

The sheer white curtains over her bedroom window fluttered in a light breeze. She let her eyes wander slowly around the room. It was still unfamiliar to her. Everything was so clean. So bright. So . . . *nice*.

The hospital cot had been narrow and hard. The nurses tucked the scratchy sheets in so tightly, Jenny had trouble getting under them.

Jenny dropped onto her soft bedspread, remembering.

In the hospital, she had shared a room with five other girls. No privacy. Some of them, she remembered, cried at night. Every night.

The phone rang, jolting Jenny from her unhappy memories.

She glanced at the bed table clock. Nearly midnight.

Who would be calling this late?

*Mr. Hagen!*

She couldn't help it. She couldn't keep the frightening memories from flooding back.

Mr. Hagen. He had always called so late. In his cruel, raspy whisper. *"Company's coming, Babes."* The cold, terrifying threat.

*"Company's coming."*

The phone rang again. So loud in the deep silence of the house.

Jenny reached for the receiver.

She hesitated.

Should she pick it up?

# Chapter 3

*It's not going to be Mr. Hagen!* she told herself.

I'm not going to be afraid to pick up the phone ever again.

She grabbed the receiver before it could ring a third time and raised it to her ear. "Hello?"

"Hi, Jen."

"Claire?"

"Yeah. It's me."

"What's wrong, Claire?" Jenny asked. "Why are you — "

"Just wondered if you were okay," Claire replied. She yawned loudly.

"Well, of course," Jenny told her. "I'm fine. I don't understand — "

"I called a few minutes ago, and you didn't answer," Claire said sleepily. "So I got kind of worried. I mean, Rick and I dropped you off at least half an hour ago. So I figured — "

Jenny laughed. "I was out front. With Cal."

Silence at Claire's end. Then: "Oh. I see."

"He had to work late. That's why he didn't meet us," Jenny explained. "He was waiting when I got home, and . . ." Her voice trailed off.

"Okay. Sorry. I was just a little worried," Claire replied. "How come your mom didn't answer the phone?"

"You know what a heavy sleeper she is," Jenny told her. "She once slept through a tornado. Really!"

"Well . . . okay," Claire said. "I — I just wanted to say it was great. I mean, tonight, Jen. I mean, it's just so great having you back. Really."

"Thanks, Claire," Jenny choked out. She felt a wave of emotion sweep over her. "You're a good friend. But I don't want you to worry about me. I'm going to be fine. From now on."

"I know," Claire replied softly. "But, listen, Jen. If there's anything . . . anything stressing you out, or anything messing up your mind. Anything you want to talk about . . . well . . . you know you can talk to me — right?"

"Thanks, Claire," Jenny repeated. "You've been great."

She said good night and hung up the phone.

A few minutes later, she clicked off the light and settled into her soft, clean, comfortable bed. Her head sank into the soft down pillow.

Before I was in the hospital, she realized, I never noticed things like a pillow or a soft bed. I took everything for granted. Everything. But, now, everything makes me happy. All the little things I never noticed — they all make me happy.

Jenny was about to drift into sleep when she heard the first howl.

It's the wind through the trees, she told herself drowsily.

The second howl made her sit up.

An animal howl. Filled with anger. And pain.

She lowered her feet to the floor. Turned toward the window, to the fluttering curtains. Listened intently.

Another long, low animal howl.

Jenny shivered. "What's making that cry?" she wondered out loud.

She stood up and tiptoed to the window.

# Chapter 4

Pushing the curtains aside, Jenny poked her head out of the window and peered down.

White moonlight washed over the backyard, making the lawn gleam like silver. A large green watering can lay on its side near her mother's flower garden. The garden hose sat coiled like a snake beside the garage wall.

Another low howl.

So cold. So hollow-sounding.

Jenny lowered her eyes toward it.

And caught a glimpse of someone. Or something. Flitting across the grass.

A boy?

Blond hair?

A little boy?

Huh?

A wind gust blew the curtain over her face. The soft fabric tickled her skin. She pulled the curtain away with both hands.

Peered down.

No one there now.

No blond-haired boy.

No one. Nothing moving. And not a sound. Except for faint music. Someone playing music several houses away.

No howls. No boy scampering across the back lawn.

Jenny, you always had a good imagination, she told herself.

Letting the curtains slide over her, she turned and strode back to bed.

She met the Warsaw kids the next afternoon.

A sultry summer day. The grass felt hot and dry beneath her bare feet. Jenny wore a faded pink midriff top and denim cutoffs cut very short. She had tied her brown hair up in a bun to keep it off her back.

Carrying a can of iced tea and a paperback mystery novel, she made her way to the broad sassafras tree in the middle of the backyard. She settled in the shade, leaning her back against the smooth tree trunk, and set the iced-tea can beside her on the grass.

Two black-and-yellow monarch butterflies fluttered over the geraniums in her mother's garden. It was a lot cooler beneath the tree,

Jenny realized happily. And the grass smelled fragrant and sweet.

Jenny heard a metallic jangle. The jangle of dog tags. A big German shepherd poked its head out from the side of the garage.

"How are you, boy?" Jenny called.

She had seen the dog before. He lived across the street. He lumbered over, his bushy tail wagging. He let Jenny stroke his back for a few seconds. Then he wandered off toward the front of the house.

She gazed around the backyard contentedly. The watering can on its side and the coiled garden hose brought back the memory of the night before. The strange howls. The little blond boy.

But the memory had lost its fear for Jenny.

I was half-asleep, she told herself. I probably heard someone's TV. I didn't see a boy in the yard. I saw shadows, tossed by the wind.

The first thing Jenny had learned in the hospital was not to frighten herself.

As soon as she had learned that, as soon as she had learned to lock her mind on cold reality, to keep her mind from creating its own horrors — she started to recover.

Even the nightmares had stopped.

What haunting, chilling nightmares she had

suffered through! Stomach-churning scenes of Mr. Hagen pulling himself up from the grave. Mr. Hagen. Staggering toward Jenny, his skeletal hands outstretched, the decaying skin falling off in clumps from his eyeless skull.

Hideous, hideous dreams — dreams so real, they had made Jenny wake up shrieking, drenched in cold sweat, morning after morning.

But no more.

Not a single nightmare.

Because she lived in the real world now.

Jenny took a long sip of the iced tea. She rubbed the cold can against her temples. Then she set it down beside her and opened her book.

A high-pitched giggle from the next yard made her turn her eyes to the fence. A white picket fence separated the Jefferses' new house from the neighbors'.

The fence needed a paint job, Jenny saw. The paint was faded and peeling. A few of the boards were cracked and tilting at odd angles.

Jenny heard another laugh. Then excited cries.

Kids. A boy and a girl? Two boys?

Jenny's mom had reported that new neighbors had moved into the house next door. But Jenny hadn't met them yet.

She felt tempted to get up and go peer over the fence. But she was too comfortable. She raised the book and started to read.

She had read only a paragraph when she heard her name being called. "Jenny? Are you Jenny?"

Gazing up, Jenny saw a woman leaning on the fence from the next yard. She had her arms resting on the fence. Her face was round, circled by tight ringlets of light brown hair.

"Are you Jenny?" the woman repeated. She had a tiny, little girl's voice. Sort of a cartoon voice, Jenny thought. Jenny couldn't guess her age. Somewhere between thirty and forty.

"Uh . . . hi." Jenny climbed slowly to her feet, being careful not to spill the iced tea.

"I'm Mrs. Warsaw," the woman said. "I met your mother, but I haven't met you."

Jenny heard angry shouts from behind the fence. The kids were fighting about something. Mrs. Warsaw turned away to break it up.

When the angry shouting ended, the woman turned back to Jenny. "Nice to meet you," Jenny said awkwardly. "It's such a hot day, I — " She motioned to the tree.

"Can you do me a favor?" Mrs. Warsaw asked. She brushed a fly off her face with a chubby hand. The sun made the tight ringlets around her face gleam.

"A favor?" Jenny asked. She took a few steps closer to the fence. The grass felt hot beneath her bare feet.

"I have to run to the store," Mrs. Warsaw said, turning to glance back at the kids. "Could you come over here and watch them for a few minutes?"

More shouts.

The woman turned to the kids again. "Sean. Meredith. What are you doing now?"

Jenny swallowed hard.

She's asking me to baby-sit, she realized. She struggled to fight the dread away, to fight back the memories that threatened to invade her mind.

"I'll be back in five minutes," Mrs. Warsaw promised in her tiny mouse voice. "Ten or fifteen at the most. I'm really sorry to trouble you. But there's no one else I can ask."

"Well . . ." Jenny hesitated.

Mrs. Warsaw sighed. "I can't really afford a full-time baby-sitter. You understand. I'm usually home during the day. So it's no problem. But, today . . ."

Jenny took a deep breath. "I'll come right over," she said.

"Oh, thanks! Thanks so much! You're a doll!" Mrs. Warsaw cried gratefully. "They're good kids. They'll just play outside till I get back. Thanks, Jenny. I really appreciate it."

"No problem," Jenny murmured.

She picked up her iced-tea can and started to make her way around the fence.

I'm baby-sitting, she thought.

My troubles always started when I was baby-sitting.

But it's only for ten minutes.

I'll be fine. I'll be perfectly fine.

*Won't I?*

# Chapter 5

Jenny stepped into the Warsaws' yard. Mrs. Warsaw had already climbed into her car, a green Taurus.

"Sean! Meredith! Don't fight!" she called. "Be nice to Jenny, okay?" She slammed the car door shut and backed down the gravel driveway.

Jenny turned to the kids. Sean was eight or nine. He was skinny and pale, almost frail-looking. He stared at Jenny through large brown eyes. Solemn eyes.

Sean's white-blond hair fell carelessly down to his collar. He wore an oversized T-shirt and baggy denim shorts, which made him look even skinnier.

Meredith squeezed a yellow tennis ball between her chubby hands. She was five or six, plump, with a round face like her mother's. She had curly, light brown hair tied back in a loose ponytail, and tiny dark eyes close together around a pudgy stub of a nose.

Meredith wore a sleeveless yellow T-shirt and matching yellow shorts. Her sneakers were yellow, too.

She's not very pretty, Jenny thought, staring back at her.

Meredith had a red scratch across one chubby knee. She had a small Band-Aid on her chin. Beads of sweat glistened above her upper lip.

"Hi, guys," Jenny greeted them cheerfully. "What's up?"

Sean pointed. "You're barefoot."

Jenny nodded, glancing down at her feet. "Yeah. I know."

"Mom says it's dangerous to go barefoot," Sean declared. "You could step on something and cut your foot."

"I cut *my* foot last summer," Meredith announced, squeezing the tennis ball in her hand. She slapped at a horsefly on the back of her left leg. "Ow!"

"I'll be careful," Jenny told them. "It's such a hot day, I thought — "

The screen door slammed. Jenny turned to the back of the house in time to see another boy step out of the kitchen.

"Here comes Seth," Sean said.

"Hey — he's your twin!" Jenny exclaimed.

Sean nodded.

Jenny saw at once that Sean and Seth were identical twins. Seth had the same white-blond hair, the same solemn, brown eyes. He had the same slender, frail build, the same pale skin.

He came running up to Jenny and smiled at her. "Hi, I'm Seth." His voice was softer than Sean's, younger somehow.

"I'm Jenny," she greeted him. She glanced quickly from one boy to the other. "How can I tell you guys apart?"

"You can't," Sean replied casually.

Seth laughed. Sean's expression remained stern.

Sean isn't terribly friendly, Jenny thought. Maybe he's shy.

"Do you live next door?" Seth asked, pointing to the fence.

Jenny nodded. "Yeah." She turned to the Warsaws' house. It was a white clapboard box, two stories high, with a small attic. A gray slate roof with an old TV antenna still clinging to the chimney.

"Do you like your new house?" Jenny asked the kids.

"No," Meredith and Sean replied in unison.

Jenny laughed. "Why not?"

"Because it's haunted," Sean told her.

Was he making a joke? Jenny waited for him to smile. But Sean's expression remained as serious as ever.

"Sean believes in ghosts," Seth said, grinning. "He's kind of spooky."

"It *is* haunted!" Meredith insisted. "The house is haunted, and you know it, Seth!"

"Shut up, Piggy!" Sean shouted at his sister.

"*You* shut up!" Meredith shot back in a shrill whine. "And don't call me Piggy!"

Seth smiled up at Jenny. "They always fight like that," he explained to her. "No big deal."

Meredith glared angrily at Sean. Then she turned to Jenny, a devilish grin spreading over her round face. "When Sean was little, Mommy used to call him Bunny Rabbit."

"Shut up!" Sean screamed. "I mean it, Meredith! Shut up!"

Meredith's grin grew wider. She ignored her brother and kept her gaze on Jenny. "Mommy called him Bunny Rabbit because he was so tiny and pale, he looked like a little bunny rabbit."

Meredith let out a mean laugh.

Sean's face turned bright pink. "I said *shut up!*" he screamed.

He dove at Meredith angrily.

Still laughing, she ducked away and started to run.

With an angry cry, Sean ran after her. He caught her easily. Tackled her from behind. Landed on top of her. And began furiously pounding her back with both fists.

Thrashing her arms helplessly, Meredith started to scream and cry.

"Hey — stop!" Jenny shouted, running over to them.

Seth got there first. He struggled to pull his brother away. "Whoa. Come on. Whoa!" he urged.

Jenny slid her hands under Sean's armpits and lifted him off his sister. "Stop it, Sean!" she insisted. "Calm down — okay?" He feels so light, Jenny thought. Like picking up a feather pillow.

Meredith climbed to her feet and rubbed at the grass stains on her knees. "Sean, you're so dumb," she muttered.

Jenny set Sean back down on his feet. "You shouldn't hit your sister like that," she scolded.

"I didn't hurt her!" Sean protested angrily. He walked across the grass and picked up the tennis ball.

"Hey — that's mine!" Meredith called.

Seth stepped up close to Jenny. "They do this all the time," he said softly. "But it's no big deal. Really."

"Aren't they ever nice to each other?" Jenny whispered.

"Sometimes," Seth replied, flashing her a sweet smile. He trotted across the grass to play catch with Sean.

The twins are certainly different, Jenny thought. She felt drawn to Seth immediately. He seemed so sweet and calm. And kind.

Jenny studied Sean. Lots of brothers don't get along with their little sisters, she knew. But Sean seemed so angry, so ready to explode at any moment. He started screaming for Meredith to shut up before she had hardly said a word.

Why was Meredith so eager to tell that Bunny Rabbit story about Sean? Jenny wondered. Why was she so eager to embarrass Sean and make him angry?

Jenny sighed.

Kids, she thought.

Kids are definitely weird.

The twins were playing catch, tossing the tennis ball as high as they could, sending high fly balls to each other across the yard.

"Give me my ball back!" Meredith demanded. She ran into Sean — charging like a bull — and made him miss the ball. Then the two of them scrambled over the grass to grab it.

"Hey, I've got an idea!" Jenny called. She reached out her hands. "Toss me the ball. We'll play a game. All of us. Okay?"

"Cool!" Seth cried with enthusiasm.

"What kind of game?" Sean asked skeptically.

Jenny taught them how to play Slap Ball. She was the pitcher. She bounced the tennis ball — one bounce — to the batter, who slapped the ball with an open hand. Since they didn't have enough players for teams, they just took batting practice.

The three kids liked the game. They all got along really well.

Jenny felt almost sorry when Mrs. Warsaw returned a few minutes later. She was just starting to warm up to the kids and feel comfortable with them.

Seth and Meredith seem to like me, Jenny realized. Sean was a tough cookie. He would still take some work.

As Mrs. Warsaw opened her car door, Seth disappeared into the house. Sean and Meredith went running to the car to greet their mother.

"How'd it go?" Mrs. Warsaw called to Jenny.

"Fine. Just fine," Jenny replied. She hurried to help Mrs. Warsaw carry her groceries into the house.

"Jenny's nice," Meredith told her mother.

Mrs. Warsaw turned to Sean. "Do you like Jenny, too?"

Sean shrugged his slender shoulders. "She's okay."

Mrs. Warsaw winked at Jenny. "High praise," she commented.

Jenny laughed. She carried a grocery bag into the kitchen and set it down on the counter. Then she glanced around the room. The kitchen was cluttered and cramped. The flowery wallpaper had faded, and one corner curled down from the ceiling over the stove.

A small, black table radio on the counter had been left on, tuned low to a country station. Dirty dish towels had been tossed in a pile beside it.

When the groceries had all been brought in, Jenny turned to go.

"Wait. Let me pay you," Mrs. Warsaw insisted, grabbing Jenny's arm.

"Huh? Pay me?" The thought caught Jenny by surprise. "No way, Mrs. Warsaw. It was just fifteen minutes. You really don't have to — "

"But I want to," the woman replied, picking

up one of the soiled dish towels and folding it.

"No. Really." Jenny backed to the kitchen door. "I won't take any money."

Mrs. Warsaw picked up another towel and started to fold it. "Well, next time," she said. She set down the towel. "At least let me get you a cold drink. A soda or something."

"Uh . . . okay. That would be great!" Jenny replied. "It's so hot out there. We were playing ball, and — "

"The kids really seem to like you," Mrs. Warsaw said, pulling open the refrigerator door and bending to reach the soda cans.

A loud scream from the front of the house made her pull herself up straight. "Mommy — he's *hitting* me again!" Meredith's shrill wail rose through the house like a police siren.

"Be right back." Shaking her head, Mrs. Warsaw hurried out of the kitchen to go stop the battle.

Jenny leaned one hand on the counter. The voice on the radio was announcing the weather forecast. More of the same. Hot and humid. Behind her, she could hear Mrs. Warsaw scolding the kids somewhere at the other end of the house.

A cloud rolled over the sun. The room darkened.

Jenny turned to the kitchen window. Staring

out, she could see her house rising up on the other side of the fence. I wonder if Mom is home from work, Jenny thought.

She was still staring out the window when she felt the icy hand on the back of her neck. Felt the cold, cold fingers slide wetly down her back.

# Chapter 6

With a startled cry, Jenny spun around.

"Huh?"

No one there.

She shivered. She could still feel the cold on her back.

She could still feel the wet fingers sliding around her neck.

"Hey — who did that?" she cried in a shaky voice. She rubbed the back of her neck, trying to smooth the lingering cold away. Then she ducked down and peered around the side of the counter.

Expecting to see Sean. Or Seth. Or even Meredith.

But no. No one there.

She could hear the kids arguing with their mother in the other room. It couldn't have been them.

So who touched me? Jenny asked herself.

Who slid that cold hand down my back?

She stood up. Her eyes searched the small kitchen one more time. Such a cold feeling still there, she realized. A cold presence.

Feeling shaken, she made her way to the screen door. "Mrs. Warsaw — " she called loudly. "I have to go home now! Bye!"

Jenny pushed the door open and ran out into the yard. The door slammed behind her. The yard was bathed in shade. Clouds rolled rapidly overhead. As if speeded up. As if set into fast forward.

Jenny blinked, waiting for her eyes to adjust. She turned back to the house.

And saw a face staring out at her.

A face up at the top of the house. In the narrow attic window.

"Wh-who's that?" she stammered out loud.

A boy? A girl?

She could see dark eyes. See a forehead topped by dark hair.

Not one of the kids, she thought.

Not anyone I've seen before.

Who could be up in the attic? Who could be up there staring down at me like that?

Bright sunlight rolled over the lawn, sweeping away the shade. Sunlight filled the attic window. Made it gleam like gold.

Jenny shielded her eyes.

When the light faded, she raised her eyes once more to the window.

The face had vanished.

Only darkness up there now.

A trick of the light? Jenny wondered, standing in the middle of the yard, squinting up at the narrow window.

Just light and shadows — like the man in the moon?

Or was it a real face I saw? Someone staring down at me, watching me so intently.

# Chapter 7

"I'm fine," Jenny said.

"Glad to hear it." Dr. Simonson flashed her a smile and motioned to the leather couch. "You look really well, Jenny. Have you been getting some sun?"

"Just in the backyard," Jenny replied. She settled on to the couch. Her eyes went to the framed diplomas on the wall behind Dr. Simonson's desk.

The psychiatrist pushed a strand of gray hair off her forehead as she lowered herself into her desk chair. She was a small, pleasant woman, in her early sixties. Jenny had come to love her soft, soothing voice, her large blue sympathetic eyes. Her thoughtfulness. Her calm.

Someday I'd like to be calm like her, Jenny often thought. I'd like to pause and take a moment to think before saying anything. I'd like to be wise like Dr. Simonson. And kind.

"How is your mother doing?" Dr. Simonson asked, turning pages on her writing pad.

"Okay," Jenny replied. "She's very glad to have me back."

"I should think so!" the doctor exclaimed. She leaned forward, her eyes studying Jenny. "So? Anything to tell me? Problems? Dreams?"

Jenny shook her head. "No bad dreams. Not one."

Dr. Simonson smiled and nodded her head. She glanced at her desk clock. "Tell me about your week. Try to make it interesting. I just had a session with my most boring patient. She insists on telling me about her ingrown toenails!"

Jenny laughed. "Maybe she thinks you're a foot doctor."

"Maybe I *am* a foot doctor!" Dr. Simonson joked. "Heads. Feet. What's the difference?"

Jenny took a deep breath and tried to recall all that had happened to her in the past week. She talked about Claire. And Rick. And Cal. About getting used to her new house. And about baby-sitting for the new kids next door.

That aroused Dr. Simonson's interest. She set down her pen and studied Jenny. "How did that go?"

"Fine," Jenny told her with a shrug. "The kids don't get along that well. But they're okay."

"You felt comfortable?" the doctor asked.

Jenny thought about it. "Yes. Fine."

Dr. Simonson gave her an approving nod. "Sounds good, Jenny. It all sounds good." She cleared her throat. Checked the clock again. "So what scared you this week?"

"Excuse me?" The question caught Jenny by surprise.

"What scared you, Jenny? There must have been something."

"When I was alone in the Warsaws' kitchen, I felt a presence. A cold presence. I felt cold fingers on the back of my neck. When I turned around, there was no one there. And when I went outside, I saw someone up in the attic, someone I had never seen before, staring down at me."

Those were the words Jenny *wanted* to say.

Those were the words that were about to burst out.

But she held them back. She forced herself not to say them.

She didn't want to tell Dr. Simonson about the icy hand, the strange face in the attic.

She didn't want to tell Dr. Simonson anything to make her think that Jenny wasn't one hundred percent okay.

Because I *am* okay, Jenny told herself. And no one is going to tell me that I'm not.

"I'm fine," she told Dr. Simonson, returning the doctor's unblinking stare. "Perfectly fine. Nothing scared me this week. Nothing at all."

After her doctor appointment, Jenny drove to the community pool and visited Claire. It was a cloudy day, threatening rain. Jenny found the pool nearly empty. There were few customers for the food stand, so Claire had plenty of time to talk.

It started to drizzle a little before five. A warm, summer rain that made the air heavy and steamy.

Jenny drove to the mall and picked up a few items her mother had asked for. She thought about dropping into the shoe store to visit Rick. But it was nearly dinnertime. She didn't want to keep her mother waiting.

At a little after six, she pulled the car into the garage. She made her way into the kitchen to find Mrs. Warsaw seated at the counter, finishing a cup of tea.

Jenny's mom hurried over to take the packages from Jenny's arms. "Did you get soaked?" she asked.

Jenny cheerfully shook her head. "The rain felt good, actually."

"Good timing," Mrs. Warsaw declared, shoving the cup and saucer away. "I was just asking your mom if you can stay with the kids tonight."

Jenny turned to her mom. "Baby-sit?"

Mrs. Jeffers bit her lower lip. Her dark eyes locked on Jenny. "Only if you feel like it."

"I won't be out late," Mrs. Warsaw added. "I know this is so last minute. But I couldn't find anyone else."

"I'll be right next door," Mrs. Jeffers told Jenny. "If anything happens, I'm five seconds away."

Jenny hesitated.

Her mother stared at her with concern. "But if it will make you uncomfortable, dear . . . feel free to say no. I'm sure Mrs. Warsaw will understand."

"The kids really liked you," Mrs. Warsaw said. She pulled a thread off her pink and blue sundress. "They begged me to get you to stay with them."

"It's up to you, Jen. Really," her mother insisted.

Jenny turned to Mrs. Warsaw. "What time do you need me?"

A smile burst across Mrs. Warsaw's round face. "Seven o'clock?"

"See you then," Jenny replied.

*You'll be okay,* she told herself.

*You'll be okay from now on.*

It's just a baby-sitting job, Jenny thought.

What could happen?

# Chapter 8

"They won't let me play!" Meredith whined. "Make them give me a turn!"

The twins had hooked the Super-Nintendo to the TV in the living room and were intensely involved in a video hockey game.

"Can't you turn it down a little?" Jenny pleaded.

The volume was turned way up. The synthetic game music repeated endlessly, competing with the *slap slap slap* of the puck.

"Did you boys hear me?"

They continued feverishly maneuvering their controllers, ignoring her.

Jenny climbed up from the armchair and strode to the TV set, blocking their view.

"Hey — !"

"Move away!"

"Are you going to give Meredith a turn?" Jenny demanded, refusing to budge.

"Meredith doesn't like hockey," Sean replied. Jenny knew it was Sean from his voice, harsher, deeper than Seth's. And because Sean was always the one being nasty to Meredith.

Otherwise, there really was no way to tell them apart. Tonight the boys were even dressed alike, in oversized dark blue T-shirts and faded denim cutoffs.

"Let me play one of *my* games!" Meredith insisted.

"Your games are too babyish," Sean replied. He frantically waved both hands, trying to persuade Jenny to move out of the way.

"You can have a turn when the hockey game is over," Seth suggested.

"Well, hurry up!" Meredith demanded.

Jenny stepped away from the front of the TV. "That was nice of you, Seth," she said, patting his blond head as she made her way past the boys to the armchair.

"Seth is a *nice* boy!" Sean declared sarcastically. He reached over and tickled his twin in the ribs. "Nice boy! Such a nice boy!"

Seth jerked out of Sean's reach. He continued moving his controller. A cheer went up on the screen. The music played a fanfare.

"Goal!" Seth screamed. "Goal!" He stuck his tongue out at Sean.

"It doesn't count!" Sean declared angrily. "I was tickling you. I wasn't watching!"

"It counts!" Seth argued. "You lose. You lose big."

Jenny dropped back into the armchair. She turned to Meredith. "I forgot to ask your mom about bedtimes. When do you guys go to bed?"

"Seth and I go at midnight!" Sean replied, grinning at Seth. "Meredith's bedtime is *now*!"

"It is not!" Meredith protested. "You're a jerk, Sean."

"You're a bigger jerk!" Sean shot back.

Jenny raised both hands in a "halt" sign. "Come on, guys," she pleaded. "I asked a simple question. When is bedtime?"

"I go at eight-thirty," Meredith told her. "Sean and Seth — they go at nine." And then she added, "But they never do."

Jenny laughed. For some reason, Meredith's serious expression struck her funny. Before long, they were all laughing. Jenny wasn't sure why. But they all started laughing at once, and couldn't stop.

She had fun with them for the rest of the evening.

They played several long games of *Uno*. Meredith had trouble keeping the rules of the card game straight, but Jenny helped her. And for once, Sean wasn't mean to her.

Jenny gave them all ice-cream bars for a late snack.

They watched a little TV, channel-surfing from station to station, not finding anything the kids were interested in.

And then Jenny managed to get them upstairs to their bedrooms by nine-thirty.

Meredith had a tiny pink room, no bigger than a clothes closet. Her bed stretched across the back of the room under the window. One entire wall contained built-in shelves up to the ceiling. They were jammed with books, and games, and dozens of dolls and stuffed animals.

Jenny tucked her in and clicked off the overhead light. Then she made her way down the hall to the twins' room. Their room wasn't much larger, just big enough to hold bunk beds, a small desk, and a dresser.

Jenny reached to turn out the light.

"I'm not tired," Sean insisted. "I want to stay up later."

"Get into bed," Jenny replied sternly. "It's late, Sean."

"But I'm not tired!" he protested.

"I'm tired," Seth said, yawning. He was already tucked into the upper bunk. "Come on, Sean. Give Jenny a break."

Sean reluctantly obeyed his brother.

Seth is such a good kid, Jenny thought gratefully. He's been so sweet.

She clicked out the light and turned to leave their bedroom — when she heard the sound.

A creaking. Overhead.

Swallowing hard, Jenny stopped in the doorway, half in the bedroom, half in the dimly lit hall.

And listened.

She heard it again. Floorboards creaking.

First one direction. Then back.

Footsteps.

Feeling a chill of fright, she raised her eyes to the ceiling.

And heard the sound again.

Someone is up there, Jenny realized, gripped with fear.

Someone is up in the attic.

# Chapter 9

Jenny turned back to the boys. "Did you hear anything?" she asked in a trembling voice.

They both sat up. "Hear what?" Sean demanded.

"Uh . . ." Jenny hesitated. She didn't want to frighten them.

But then the ceiling groaned. The footsteps were right overhead.

"Did you hear that?" Jenny blurted out. "Up in the attic?"

"It's nothing," Seth assured her. "We always hear noises at night — don't we, Sean?"

"Yeah," his brother agreed, yawning.

"Are you scared, Jenny?" Seth asked softly.

"No," Jenny answered quickly.

What am I doing? she scolded herself. I don't want to scare the boys because the ceiling is creaking.

"Uh . . . good night, guys," she said, turning into the hall. "Sweet dreams."

She took a few steps along the narrow hallway. Then she stopped and listened again.

*Creak . . . creeeeeak . . .*

There's someone walking back and forth up there, Jenny decided.

She took a deep breath and held it. I'm not going to let my fear run away with me, she told herself. She remembered the important lessons she had learned in the hospital.

She fought back the panic that froze her.

I'm in charge here, she told herself. I'm in control.

She gazed around the narrow hallway. A single dim floor lamp at the other end of the hall provided the only light. The shadow of a narrow table stretched across the carpet like two bony arms.

*Creeeeeak . . . creak . . .*

Maybe an animal climbed into the attic, she decided.

A squirrel. Or a raccoon.

She remembered the time a squirrel had somehow found its way into the attic in her old house. Jenny was a little girl. Her father was still living with them. He chased after the squirrel with a fishing net.

Every time Mr. Jeffers swung the net, the

squirrel darted away. Back and forth, her father chased the squirrel through the cluttered attic. Furniture crashed to the floor. A pile of cartons toppled over.

Her father went into a rage, screaming at the squirrel, swinging the net wildly. And the angrier he got, the harder Jenny laughed.

He just looked so funny. A big bear of a man chasing after a tiny, scrawny, frightened squirrel.

Finally, Jenny remembered, when the attic was totally destroyed and her father was red-faced and gasping for air, the squirrel casually hopped out the window and disappeared.

Recalling that long-ago day brought a smile to Jenny's face.

*Creeeeak. Creeeak.*

The sounds above her head snapped her from her memories. It's just a squirrel, she decided. I'm not afraid. I'll go check it out.

She crossed the hall to the doorway that led up to the attic.

She reached for the glass doorknob.

And felt a bony hand slide against her waist.

# Chapter 10

"Ohhh!"

Jenny uttered a startled cry.

She turned to see one of the twins staring up at her.

"Sean — !" she cried. "You scared me! I — "

"I'm Seth," he said softly. "I'm sorry, Jenny. I thought you heard me."

He appeared so small, so pale, in the dim hall light. His pajama sleeves hung down over his hands.

"I — I was just going to check out the attic," Jenny told him shakily, still struggling to catch her breath.

"No, you can't," he replied, his voice just above a whisper.

Jenny stared down at him in surprise. "Huh? Why not?"

"It's locked," he told her. He grabbed the glass knob and turned it. "See? Mom keeps it locked. No one is allowed to go up there."

Jenny tried the door, too. Seth was right. The door was locked.

"But why?" she asked him.

"It's too dangerous," Seth replied quickly. He scratched his thick, blond hair.

*Creeeeeak . . . creeeeak.*

Jenny gasped. The footsteps sounded so near.

She raised her eyes to the ceiling.

"It's okay," Seth said. He didn't appear at all frightened or concerned.

Jenny turned back to him. "Too dangerous? Seth — what do you mean?"

He shrugged his slender shoulders. "I think the stairs are broken or something. Or maybe the attic floor. Mom said it was too dangerous. So she locked the door."

How weird, Jenny thought, glancing back up to the creaking ceiling.

Or maybe it wasn't weird at all. Maybe the attic stairs really were in bad repair. The Warsaws had just moved in a few weeks before. Mrs. Warsaw wouldn't have had time to have them fixed.

*Creeeeeak.*

Jenny decided to ignore the creaks and
groans. Seth wasn't the least bit afraid of them.
So why should she be afraid?

"Let me tuck you in again," she said softly.
She placed a hand on his shoulder and guided
him back to his room. "Hey, Seth — where's
your dad?" The question blurted out. Since
she had met the family, Jenny had been wondering where Mr. Warsaw was.

"He died," Seth replied, without any emotion at all.

"Oh. I'm sorry," Jenny said. She shook her
head. *Why did I ask that question now? Why
do these things pop into my head?*

Seth climbed back up to the top bunk. *Sean
must already be asleep,* Jenny told herself. He
didn't stir. "Good night, Seth," she whispered.
"Sweet dreams."

She saw him pull the blanket up to his head.
"Night, Jenny." A tiny whisper. Like a mouse
squeak.

Ignoring the sounds from the attic, Jenny
made her way downstairs. She pulled a diet
Coke from the refrigerator, then settled into
the living room armchair to read the book she
had brought.

After a few paragraphs, the words blurred
on the page. *I'm not in the mood,* she decided.

She shut the book and dropped it to the floor.

She took a long sip from the soda can, listening for the creaking sounds. But she couldn't hear them from downstairs.

The phone rang. She set down the soda can and picked up the receiver. "Hello. Warsaws'."

"Jenny?"

"Oh, hi, Claire." Jenny felt glad to hear her friend's voice.

"Your mom said you were baby-sitting next door," Claire said. "She gave me the number. How's it going?"

"Okay. Good!" Jenny declared. "No problem."

"Does it feel kind of weird to be baby-sitting again?" Claire asked.

"Kind of," Jenny replied. "But I'm okay. Really. The kids are pretty good. They're all in bed."

"So you have time to talk?" Claire asked. "I heard some great gossip today. About Ashley Franklin and Gary Wilson."

Jenny chuckled. "Spill."

She and Claire talked and gossiped for nearly half an hour. The relaxed conversation made Jenny feel good.

I'm back to normal, she thought. Back to a

normal life. Back to myself again.

Then, a few minutes later, the phone rang again.

And Jenny heard the voice she hoped never to hear again.

The whispered, raspy voice that had filled her life with so much horror.

*"Hi, Jenny,"* he whispered. *"Hi, Jenny — it's me."*

# Chapter 11

A low moan escaped Jenny's throat.

She gripped the phone so hard, her hand ached.

Mr. Hagen is dead, she reminded herself. He can't be calling me.

He can't.

The frightening phone calls had been the beginning of Jenny's troubles. Two nights a week, she had baby-sat for the Hagens' little boy. But then the whispered calls started: *"Company's coming, Babes."*

Calls from Mr. Hagen. He was crazy. He hated baby-sitters. All baby-sitters. He called Jenny again and again. Frightening, whispered calls.

And now she heard the terrifying whisper again in her ear.

*"Hi, Jenny. It's me."*

"Who — who is this?" Jenny demanded.

*"It's me. Cal."*

"Huh?" She nearly dropped the phone. "Cal? You — you scared me," she stammered. "Why are you whispering like that?"

"I can barely talk," Cal rasped. "Laryngitis. I have the *worst* sore throat."

Jenny let out a long, relieved sigh. She slumped back in the armchair. "I — I thought — "

"How's it going?" Cal whispered.

Jenny had to laugh. "It was going okay till you called. That scary whisper — it really frightened me."

"Sorry," Cal replied. "I always get bad sore throats like this. Listen, let me come over and make it up to you."

"I don't think so," Jenny replied. She wrapped the phone cord around her wrist, then unwrapped it.

"I won't stay long," he told her. "Half an hour. Then I'll go. Promise."

"It's not a good idea," Jenny replied.

"It's an excellent idea," he whispered.

"You're sick — remember? You shouldn't go out."

"I'm not sick," Cal protested. "I just have laryngitis." He suddenly sounded hurt. "Don't you *want* to see me?"

"Of course I want to see you," Jenny replied.

"Then why can't I come over there?"

She giggled. "Because you're bad."

"Who? Me?"

"You're bad," she repeated, teasing him. "You won't leave after half an hour. Mrs. Warsaw will come back home and find you here."

"No way!" he protested.

"Give me a break, Cal," Jenny said, turning serious. "This is my first night baby-sitting here. You know I can really use the money. I don't want to blow this job."

"But, Jen — " he started.

"No, Cal. N-O."

"Does that mean yes?"

She started to laugh. But a sudden chill made her stop.

A cold presence in the room. As if someone had suddenly turned the air conditioner on high.

And then Jenny felt fingers around her neck. Cold, bony fingers. From behind her.

So cold. So cold and wet.

Tightening. Tightening around her neck.

With a gasp, she dropped the phone receiver.

Then she started to scream.

"Jenny — what is it? What's happening?" She could hear Cal's raspy voice from the phone receiver on the floor.

Jenny leaped up. Spun around.

No one there. No one.

The grip of cold still tingling her neck.

She rubbed her neck with both hands, smoothing away the cold, rubbing away the feeling of bony fingers.

"Jenny — are you okay?" Cal's urgent cries from the phone at her feet. "Jenny? Answer me!"

Breathing hard, she swung herself around to the back of the big armchair.

"Who's hiding back there? Who grabbed my neck?"

No one back there.

"Who's trying to scare me?" she called, moving around the small room, searching behind the couch, examining the stairway in the front hall.

No one.

The cold lingered heavily in the room. The tingling at the back of her neck faded slowly.

Who *was* it? How did they disappear so quickly?

Shaking her head, she bent and picked up

the phone. "It's okay," she said breathlessly. "I'm okay."

"What happened?" Cal demanded, his voice even more of a hoarse croak. "I heard you scream."

"I . . . well . . ."

She didn't want to tell him. What could she say? That the room suddenly got cold and an invisible hand had grabbed her neck and started to strangle her?

If she told him that, Cal would have no choice. He would have to call Jenny's mother and tell her that Jenny was cracking up again.

"I . . . just dropped my soda can," she lied. "Call you later — okay? I'd better mop up the rug."

"Are you sure — ?" Cal started.

"Call you later." She hung up the phone.

She leaned her head against the armchair back, catching her breath.

I'm okay, she told herself. I'm perfectly okay.

She glanced around the room again. Everything in place. Everything okay.

She stood up slowly. Checked behind the chair one more time.

It's the boys, she decided. Sean and Seth. Playing a joke on me. Trying to scare me to death.

She started toward the stairs. Probably Sean, she told herself. There's something mean-natured about that one. Seth is so sweet. But Sean definitely has a cruel streak.

She thought about how mean Sean was to his sister. He was constantly teasing Meredith and doing things to show her he was boss.

Both boys look so angelic, Jenny thought with a smile. With that white-blond hair, the serious brown eyes, the pale white skin. Like perfect angels.

It's funny how two brothers can look so totally alike, Jenny thought, but still have such different personalities.

Grabbing the iron banister, she pulled herself up the stairs. I've got to tell them no more mean tricks, she told herself.

I've got to be firm with them right from the start.

No more scaring the baby-sitter. From now on, bedtime is bedtime. If I get the rules straight now, I won't have any trouble with them later.

She reached the second-floor landing, turned into the narrow hall, and strode quickly to the twins' room.

The door was closed.

That's weird, Jenny thought. After I tucked

Seth in for the second time, I remember leaving the door open.

She grabbed the handle and pushed open the door.

"Hey, guys — "

Even in the dim light from the hall, Jenny could see that they were gone.

# Chapter 12

With a trembling hand, she groped along the wall until she found the lightswitch. She clicked on the ceiling light.

The blankets on the bunk beds were tossed back. One pillow lay on the carpet.

"Seth? Sean?" Jenny called weakly. Her eyes frantically darted around the room.

She dropped to all fours and peered under the bed.

No. They weren't hiding under there.

She climbed to her feet, crossed the small room, and pulled open the closet door.

Not in there, either.

"Hey — where are you two hiding?" she called. "This isn't funny, you know."

Silence.

"Come on, guys. You're scaring me!" Jenny called. "This isn't a funny joke."

She pulled up the blankets on both beds to

make sure they weren't hiding beneath them. Then she bent down to peer under the small desk.

Not there.

Nowhere else to search in the bedroom.

She returned to the door. "Seth? Sean?"

When she heard soft giggling out in the hall, Jenny breathed a long sigh of relief. "Hey, you two — !" She strode quickly into the hallway.

More giggling. From behind a partly open door at the end of the hall.

Jenny jogged toward the sound of soft laughter. Pulled open the door. A clothes closet. Both boys peered up at her from deep in the closet. Wide grins on their faces.

"Not funny!" Jenny scolded. She reached in and pulled them out, one hand for each. They didn't resist. "Not funny!" she repeated.

They both laughed harder. "Yes, it was!" they cried in unison. They flashed each other glances and started laughing again.

Jenny dragged them out into the center of the hallway. "Listen to me, guys," she insisted. "Do you want me to come baby-sit for you again?"

"Yes," Seth replied. Sean nodded.

"Then don't scare me anymore. I really mean it."

"Why not?" Sean demanded, his eyes

gleaming mischievously. "It was just a joke."

"I don't like those kind of jokes," Jenny replied sternly. "They get me really upset."

Their grins faded. Jenny could see that she was finally getting through to them. "Now let me tuck you in," she said, softening her tone. "But from now on, when I tuck you in, you have to stay tucked in. Okay?"

They muttered agreement.

The ceiling creaked.

Jenny automatically glanced up. The boys didn't pay any attention. "Did you hear that?" she blurted out.

Sean nodded. "There's someone locked up there," he told Jenny. "A prisoner."

He grinned at Seth. Seth gave him a playful shove. Both boys uttered high-pitched giggles.

"Ha-ha. Funny joke," Jenny said sarcastically. "You guys are real funny tonight."

The ceiling creaked again. This time Jenny ignored it. She guided the boys to their room and tucked them into the bunk beds. She said good night again and clicked off the ceiling light.

Now maybe they'll go to sleep, she told herself.

She started down the stairs. But stopped a third of the way down.

She heard footsteps in the living room.

A loud crash. Glass shattering on the floor.
More footsteps. Coming closer.
Jenny gripped the iron banister.
Someone has broken in, she realized.
*Now* what do I do?

# Chapter 13

She didn't have time to do anything.

A shadow fell over the stairway. And then a tall figure stepped out of the living room.

"Huh? You?" she shrieked.

Cal raised his eyes to her. "Oh, wow! Thank goodness!" he cried in his hoarse voice. He flew up the stairs and wrapped his arms around her.

"Cal? What are you doing here?" Jenny cried breathlessly. "You — you scared me to death. I thought — "

He placed two fingers on her lips. Then, still holding her tightly, he lowered his head and kissed her.

A short kiss. Jenny pulled back quickly, eager to get some answers. "I told you *not* to come here," she said shrilly. "And then you break in, and — "

"I didn't break in," Cal replied in a raspy whisper. They both sat down on the bottom step. "The door was open a little, so I let myself in."

"But what are you *doing* here?" Jenny repeated impatiently.

"You screamed," Cal replied, taking her hand. "When I was talking to you on the phone. You sounded so frightened. I knew it wasn't just a soda can dropping. So I drove over as fast as I could."

"Cal — I really can take care of myself," Jenny replied angrily. "I know you think I'm still a total basket case. But, really — "

"That's *not* what I think!" Cal cried. He let go of her hand and jumped to his feet. "I know you're okay now, Jen. But when you screamed like that, I thought — "

"Okay, okay," Jenny replied, motioning for him to sit back down beside her. "You're right. I didn't drop a soda can. I heard something, and it startled me — okay? Big deal. That was no reason for you to come running over here and — "

"Didn't you hear me ringing the bell?" Cal demanded. "I rang and rang, and you didn't answer. So I got even more worried."

"I didn't hear it," Jenny told him. "The bell must be broken. The Warsaws just moved in.

They haven't had time to fix things up."

"When you didn't come to the door, I tried it, and it was open," Cal continued. "So I let myself in. When I saw you weren't in the living room, I started to get really scared. I started searching the house."

"I heard a crash," Jenny said. "I thought — "

"I was a little crazed," Cal admitted. "I walked right into the coffee table. I'm afraid I broke a glass vase. I — I'll help you clean it up."

"You always were a total klutz," Jenny teased. She was starting to feel better. It was nice to know that Cal cared about her enough to drop everything and come running to her like that.

He's really a great guy, she thought.

She pulled down his head with both hands and kissed him long and tenderly. As his lips moved against hers, he slid his arms around her waist and held her tight.

I feel so safe when Cal is around, Jenny thought.

But she scolded herself for thinking it. I have to feel completely safe when *I'm* the only one around, she told herself. I don't need someone else to make me feel safe.

When the kiss ended, Jenny took a moment to catch her breath. She ruffled Cal's white-blond hair. Then she grabbed both of his hands and tugged him to his feet.

They cleaned up the broken vase. Then she dragged him to the front door. "You're outta here!" she exclaimed, giving him a playful shove.

"Just a few more minutes," he pleaded, cupping his hands in a prayer position.

Jenny glanced at the clock. Just past ten-thirty.

"No way. Beat it," she insisted, giving him another shove. "Mrs. Warsaw will be home any second."

"Okay, okay," Cal grumbled. He turned at the front door. His smile faded. "You still didn't tell me why you screamed."

"Oh . . . well . . ." Jenny hesitated. She didn't want to tell him about the cold fingers on the back of her neck. She didn't want to tell him what a frightening night she'd been having before he arrived.

She shrugged. "It's just been a crazy night," she said, trying to sound light and unconcerned. "You know. Weird noises in the attic. Weird noises downstairs." She grinned at him. "A weirdo coming to visit . . ."

He smiled, but she caught his eyes staring hard at her, studying her. "You sure you're okay?"

"Cal — give me a break!" she exclaimed, pressing both hands against her waist. "Of *course* I'm okay. My house is right next door. What on earth could happen to me here?"

The phone rang about ten minutes after Cal left. Jenny had been watching TV, channel-surfing, not really paying attention to anything on the screen.

When the phone rang, she clicked off the TV. She picked up the receiver after the second ring. "Hello?"

"Hi, Jenny. It's me." Mrs. Warsaw. Jenny could hear a lot of voices in the background. People laughing. "How's it going?" Mrs. Warsaw asked, shouting over the noise.

"Fine," Jenny told her. "Just fine. The kids are asleep."

"Oh, that's great," Mrs. Warsaw replied, sounding relieved. "They usually give their baby-sitter a hard time about bedtime."

"Well, Sean and Seth were a little difficult," Jenny confessed.

"What? I'm sorry," Mrs. Warsaw shouted. "It's so noisy here. I couldn't hear you, Jenny. What about Sean?"

"Nothing. Not important," Jenny assured her. "Everything is fine."

"Well, I'm just calling to say I'll be a little

later than I thought. I should be home by eleven-thirty. That isn't a problem — is it, dear?"

"No. No problem," Jenny replied, glancing at the brass clock on the mantel.

Mrs. Warsaw shouted good-bye. Jenny heard a burst of loud laughter behind her. The line went dead.

Sounds like a good party, Jenny thought, hanging up the phone. She wondered if it was too late to call Claire.

Maybe I'd better not, she decided. Claire's dad is a light sleeper. He always gets furious if anyone calls after ten.

Jenny climbed to her feet and stretched. She walked around the room, examining the bookshelves, picking up glass and china knick-knacks.

Mrs. Warsaw seemed to have a collection of little glass animals. Jenny picked up a tiny tiger, then a tiny monkey with a curled-up tail. She rubbed her finger against the glass. So smooth.

I hope that glass vase Cal broke wasn't important to Mrs. Warsaw, Jenny thought, frowning. I hope it wasn't part of a priceless vase collection or something.

She started to pick up a china mermaid. The figurine had long, shiny red hair that rolled like an ocean wave down the length of her body to her emerald-green tail fin.

But Jenny stopped her hand in midair as she felt another wave of cold descend over the room.

She spun away from the display shelf.

No one there.

Maybe the air-conditioning clicked on, she thought. But she heard no hum. She saw no air-conditioning vent.

The cold pressed down on her, damp, clammy, heavy. She suddenly felt as if she were underwater, under a heavy, cold wave.

And then she heard a whispered voice, so close, so close to her ear:

*"Go away, Jenny."*

"Huh?" Jenny uttered a startled cry. Her eyes squinted over the small room. "Who's there?"

*"Go away, Jenny,"* the whispery voice repeated. *"Go away. Or you'll die, too."*

# Chapter 14

"Who — who's there?" Jenny stammered.

She ran to the hallway, frantically peering both ways.

No one.

"Seth? Sean?" she called.

The whispered voice was so close. The room felt so cold.

As if she had stepped into a refrigerator.

"Who said that?" Jenny cried, running to the living room window and staring out into the darkness. Then diving to the floor and searching beneath the couch, beneath the armchair.

Where? Where? Where?

She knew the answer. But she didn't want to admit it.

She knew who was whispering to her. Knew where the voice was coming from.

Coming from inside her.

Coming from inside her own head.

"No! No way!" she cried out loud.

I'm not freaking out again! she told herself. I'm not crazy!

I'm not going back to the hospital — ever again. I'm normal now, she thought, gritting her teeth, concentrating, concentrating. Trying to drive the voice away, so far away it would never come back.

I can control it, Jenny thought. Because I'm not crazy. I'm not.

*"Go away, Jenny. Go away. Or you'll die, too."*

What did that mean? I'll die, *too*?

Jenny shut her eyes. She pressed her hands against her temples.

Go away, voice. Go away.

I can will you away. I can force you away.

I am normal, normal, *normal*!

A face flashed into Jenny's thoughts. Becka. A girl she knew in the hospital. A pretty, cheerful girl with sleek, straight black hair down to her shoulders, and cold green eyes.

Becka had been ready to go home, Jenny remembered. After a long stay at the hospital, Becka had impressed the doctors enough to send her home to her parents.

Becka was a few years younger than Jenny. They had started a conversation one afternoon in the TV room. Neither of them was interested in the game shows on the TV every afternoon. So they found themselves talking, about their schools, about their families, about boys.

Most of the time, Becka was cheerful and talkative. Jenny couldn't tell why her new friend had been sent to the hospital. Whenever she brought up the subject, Becka shrugged and muttered that it was a long story.

Becka obviously didn't want to talk about it. Jenny didn't press her.

Because Jenny didn't really feel like talking about her troubles, either. About the voices she heard, the voices telling her that she was Mr. Hagen. That she was no longer Jenny. That she was now Mr. Hagen back from the grave.

And so they avoided the most important subject in their lives. And talked about movies and books they liked, vacations they had been on, normal things.

It was so important to be normal. Such an important goal.

Of course, Becka had her moody days. Her days when her green eyes lost their sparkle and she seemed to sink into herself, deep into herself. So deep that Jenny couldn't reach her.

Such a scary feeling. To be talking to someone and suddenly realize that, even though she's still sitting beside you, she's no longer there.

But the moody days grew fewer and farther apart. And then Becka seemed to be cheerful and alert whenever Jenny saw her. "I've got to get out of here," she confided to Jenny. "I'll do anything. If I spend another month in this hospital, I'll *really* crack up."

And one sunny October day, the doctors decided that Becka was normal and healthy again. What a happy day that had been.

When Becka told her the news that they were sending her home, Jenny had been so glad for her. Glad — and unhappy that she was about to lose a friend.

A few days later, Jenny crossed the hall into Becka's room to say good-bye. Becka's little sister had sent Becka a soft, brown teddy bear. On her bad days, Becka had clung to the bear, holding it tightly against her chest, refusing to let it go, even at mealtimes.

Now Jenny found Becka sitting on top of the bedcovers, in jeans and a bright pink pullover — finally out of her pale gray hospital gown.

The teddy bear rested in her lap.

Becka had ripped the head off the bear.

As Jenny stared in horror, Becka kept dipping her hand inside the bear's body, pulling out big chunks of white cotton stuffing, and eating them.

Becka still wasn't normal.

The doctors were ready to send her home. But Becka still had problems.

Standing in the middle of Mrs. Warsaw's living room, Jenny shook her head, trying to shake away her painful memories of Becka.

I'm not ready yet, either, she told herself, feeling the bitter tears brim in her eyes.

I'm just like Becka. I'm still messed up.

I'm still hearing voices. Threatening voices inside my head.

Why did the doctors let me come home? They told me I'm ready — but I'm not! I'm not!

No.

Stop it, Jenny. Stop it.

Shut up, Jenny. Take a deep breath, she instructed herself.

She dropped into the armchair and shut her eyes.

Calm down. You can figure this out, she thought.

You're not crazy. You know you're not. You're not going to *let* yourself get crazy. You're going to keep it together — no matter what it takes.

Becka's face floated into her thoughts again. And once again, Jenny saw the headless teddy bear, saw Becka hungrily swallowing the cotton stuffing.

She opened her eyes and stood up.

I'm not Becka. I'm Jenny.

And I'm not crazy. I know where the voice is coming from.

An intercom, Jenny thought. Sometimes parents have an intercom to listen in on a child's room at night.

The twins are playing another trick on me. They're using an intercom in their room to whisper that frightening message.

But where is the speaker?

Jenny frantically searched the living room. Her eyes swept over the cluttered bookshelves, over the glass vases and china animal figurines. She searched the desktop, peered on the shelf under the coffee table.

When she couldn't find an intercom speaker, she ran up the stairs to the boys' bedroom. She clicked on a ceiling light in the hall. It cast pale yellow light into the narrow room.

The boys were asleep on their backs, their covers pulled up to their chins. In the lower bunk, Sean was snoring lightly.

Are they faking? Jenny wondered. Are they pretending to sleep?

She crossed the room to the bunk beds and examined their faces. "Are you awake?" she whispered.

Neither of them moved.

Jenny turned and searched the room once again, this time looking for an intercom. Silently, she searched every surface, every shelf, every possible hiding place. She even pulled out the drawers of the desk, carefully shuffling through the contents of each drawer.

No luck.

With a dispirited sigh, she crept out of the bedroom and clicked off the hall light. Nice try, Jenny, she thought bitterly. A nice theory. But there's no intercom.

The boys are asleep. Neither one was the whisperer.

*Then who was?*

She had just stepped back into the living room when the cold whisper rasped in her ears once again.

*"Go away, Jenny. Go away NOW!"*

So close.

The dry croak of a voice so close. She could feel the rush of cold, damp air on the back of her neck. Every muscle in her body tightened. Hard goosebumps rose up and down her arms.

"Where are you?" she choked out. "Who are you? Are you inside me? Are you inside my head?"

*"Go away now, Jenny. Go away, or you'll die, too."*

# Chapter 15

"So you're not going to baby-sit anymore?" Claire asked.

Jenny shook her head. She felt embarrassed. She didn't really want to talk about it. "No. I don't think so."

"The kids were animals?" Claire asked.

"No. They were okay," Jenny replied. "It's kind of hard to explain. The house was . . . well . . . creepy."

"If you were uncomfortable there, you did the right thing," Claire said. "You shouldn't go somewhere you're uncomfortable."

Maybe I'll be uncomfortable wherever I go, Jenny thought bitterly.

"Hey, Jenny — your turn," Cal called from the bench.

"Are we going to talk, or are we going to bowl?" Rick chimed in.

"Both!" Claire called back to him.

Jenny hoisted up her bowling ball and stepped up to the lane. "Who's winning?" she called back.

"Cal is," Rick replied, glancing at the score sheet. "That's because he cheats."

"Huh? Cheat?" Cal cried in mock horror. "Give me a break! How can you cheat at bowling?"

"I can never figure out how to keep score," Claire said, pulling back her dark brown hair, fixing her ponytail. She wore an oversized white T-shirt over a sleeveless blue T-shirt and tight-fitting denim cutoffs that emphasized her long legs. "All those lines and X's."

"You don't have any X's!" Rick called, snickering. "All I see are two threes and a six!"

"At least I'm beating you!" Claire shot back.

"I have a sprained wrist," Rick replied, holding up a limp hand. "Otherwise, I'd be bowling a perfect game."

Cal motioned to Jenny. "Anytime tonight!" he called impatiently.

Jenny raised the ball to her waist and prepared to bowl. She hesitated. She could never remember whether to start her approach with her right foot or her left foot.

She took a deep breath and stepped forward. As she brought her arm forward to release the ball, it brushed the side of her jeans.

The ball bounced on to the lane, rolled straight for a few feet, then spun into the gutter.

"Not again!" she cried, raising both hands to the sides of her hair.

"Maybe you should aim for the gutter," Rick teased. "Then it might go down the alley."

"Maybe we should get that lane over there," Cal suggested, grinning. He pointed to the kiddie lane at the far side. It had bumpers down both sides so that the ball couldn't go into the gutter.

Rick laughed and slapped Cal a high five.

Claire raised her bowling ball toward the two boys. "You know, this would look really good in your mouth!" she cried.

Jenny's ball rolled back onto the rack, and she picked it up. She stepped up to the lane, made her approach, and let the ball go. This time she toppled all of the pins except for the tenpin.

"Yaaay!" She let out a cheer and clapped her hands. "Almost a spare!"

"It's called a nine," Rick said, sneering.

Laughing, Jenny stepped over to the scorers' table and gave him a hard shove. "You're a real beast, Rick," she muttered.

"But he's kind of cute," Claire chimed in.

Rick actually blushed.

Cal stepped up to take his turn. He was a

good bowler, Jenny saw. He took the game
more seriously than the other three.

Of course, Jenny knew, Cal took most
everything seriously. He didn't really like to
kid around the way most of their friends did.
He just didn't have the patience for it.

Rick left to get a Coke. Claire sat down
beside Jenny at the scorers' table. "So are you
okay?" she asked, her dark eyes probing
Jenny's.

"Huh? What do you mean?" Jenny replied,
confused.

"I mean, about the baby-sitting thing last
night," Claire explained. She pulled a string
off the shoulder of Jenny's blue-and-white
striped tank top. "What happened when that
woman came home? Mrs. . . . ?"

"Warsaw," Jenny said.

"Did you tell her you wouldn't baby-sit anymore?" Claire asked.

Jenny shook her head. "No. Not really. It
was kind of late. And I just wanted to get
home."

I wanted to get away from the cold, whispering voice, Jenny thought unhappily. But
how can I get away from it if it's inside my
head?

"So you just told her everything was fine?"
Claire continued.

"Yeah. Pretty much," Jenny said, watching Cal topple every pin except the lead pin. He scowled and tugged at his white-blond hair.

"I told her the kids were very good," Jenny said. "I said everything went okay." She sighed. "I mean, what's the point of starting a big thing? I just felt uncomfortable in the house. It kind of creeped me out. No big deal."

"Right," Claire agreed, motioning with both hands for Jenny to calm down. "You're definitely right."

Jenny hadn't realized she was shouting. She could feel her face grow hot.

Take it easy, Jenny, she warned herself. You don't want Claire to start thinking you're still a nut case.

Cal knocked the one pin down with his second ball, making his spare. "Yes!" he cried triumphantly. He flashed Jenny a smile.

Claire leaned close to Jenny. "If you do decide to go back there . . . you know . . . to baby-sit, I'll be happy to go along with you," she said quietly. "It would be kind of fun, don't you think?"

"Thanks, Claire," Jenny replied, feeling very embarrassed.

"And if you ever need to talk . . ." Claire continued, staring hard into Jenny's eyes.

"Thanks," Jenny repeated.

Claire is trying to be a good friend, Jenny told herself. But she's trying too hard.

I shouldn't have mentioned that I got a little freaked out last night. I shouldn't have mentioned that I decided not to baby-sit for Mrs. Warsaw again.

Now Claire keeps examining me like I'm some kind of lab specimen.

"It's your turn," she told Claire. "Let's see if we can beat these guys."

Cal pulled his face away. The taste of his lips lingered on hers.

Jenny pressed her forehead against his shoulder. "I had fun tonight," she said softly.

"Me, too," Cal replied. He turned from the steering wheel and shifted his arm around her. He lifted her chin with one finger and kissed her again.

When I'm with Cal, I'm okay, Jenny thought dreamily.

Cal had pulled his car halfway up her drive-way and cut the headlights. The house was dark. Jenny knew her mom went to bed pretty early on work nights.

She snuggled against Cal. "You're a pretty awesome bowler," she told him.

He snickered. "I didn't have much compe-tition tonight."

"Poor Rick!" Jenny exclaimed. "When he dropped the ball on his foot — "

"He just did that so he won't have to go to work tomorrow!" Cal interrupted.

Jenny smiled. "He hates his summer job so much."

"Why doesn't he just quit?" Cal demanded.

"He doesn't want to hurt his uncle's feelings. His uncle thinks that Rick *loves* the job. He wants to send Rick to shoe college or something!"

They both giggled.

"Rick should just quit," Cal insisted.

Jenny poked him in the ribs. "Look who's talking. You don't exactly love your job at the garage — do you?"

Cal frowned. "It's okay," he insisted. "I like messing with cars, you know. And the money isn't too bad."

Jenny saw that she had hit a sore spot. Cal didn't like to be reminded about some things. She pulled his head down and kissed him. That was the best way to get the frown off his face.

They stayed in the driveway for another half hour, talking softly, snuggling together. This is the nicest night I've had since I left the hospital, Jenny thought happily. It's the first night I've really felt relaxed.

It was nearly one in the morning when she

climbed out of Cal's car and made her way into the house. She felt sleepy and alert, relaxed and excited — all at the same time.

She turned at the door and watched Cal's car back down the driveway. He flashed on the headlights when he reached the street, then sped away.

Jenny could still taste his kisses, still feel the warmth of his arms around her. She closed the front door carefully, silently, not wanting to awaken her mother. Then she crept upstairs to her room.

She fumbled around in the darkness until she managed to click on the lamp on her bed table. Blinking as her eyes adjusted to the light, she saw a sheet of lined paper on her pillow.

A note from her mother. Jenny scooped it up and read it quickly:

*How are you? Do I ever get to see you? Or shall we just send notes? Good night. Love, Mom.*

Jenny smiled.

Constant communication. That's what her mom liked. She believed in keeping in touch all day long.

Yawning, Jenny pulled off her tank top and

jeans, leaving them in a heap on the bedroom carpet. She pulled a filmy short nightshirt from her dresser drawer and slipped it on.

The room felt hot. Jenny turned to the window and saw that it was shut. "I need some fresh air," she murmured out loud.

She crossed the room to the window and peered out. Pale moonlight washed over the backyard, making the lawn glisten.

Jenny's eyes followed the light to the Warsaws' house next door. She reached to pull open the window — then stopped.

What was that near the Warsaws' roof?

Moonlight filled the attic window.

Something moved in the silvery light.

A face. A girl's face, her dark eyes reflecting the light.

Sad eyes. A sad face.

Jenny pressed against the windowpane, staring hard.

Am I seeing things? Am I hallucinating?

No.

Jenny hurriedly pulled up the window. Pushed up the screen. And stuck her head out.

She could see the girl's face so clearly now. Dark eyes. A full, red mouth. The pretty face framed by black curls.

The girl stared out the window, stared right at Jenny.

And what were the words she was mouthing?

Jenny struggled to read the girl's lips. What was she saying?

It looked like: "Help me. Help me."

# Chapter 16

"Help me. Help me!"

Were those her words?

Jenny leaned farther out the window, struggling to see.

The backyard suddenly darkened. A cloud rolled over the moon. The dark shadow swept over the lawn, onto the Warsaws' house.

The attic window darkened to black.

The girl's face faded with it.

Jenny waited for the light to return. Down the block, she heard a car door slam. A dog barked. A gust of wind fluttered her hair.

A few seconds later, the cloud silently rolled away. The light washed over the yard, over the house next door. Filled the attic window.

But the face had vanished.

Jenny shivered, suddenly chilled. The night air was warm. But the silvery light felt so cold.

She gazed out at the empty attic window.

Waited for the sad-eyed girl to return.

Waited and watched.

Who are you, girl? Jenny wondered. Just a picture in my mind?

A face in my imagination?

No, Jenny thought. No. There's something strange at Mrs. Warsaw's house. Something strange and frightening over there.

Jenny gazed at the house through the cold, silver moonlight.

The window glowed, reflecting the light.

The girl didn't appear again.

Jenny pulled herself back into the room and went to bed.

She had a nightmare. The first one in several months.

The dream started out pleasantly. Jenny found herself in a bowling alley. She saw herself bowling easily, gracefully.

The pins toppled with a pleasant *clonk* of wood against wood.

Rick applauded. Jenny took a bow.

She bowled again. The ball felt so light. Jenny felt so light. She floated across the lane.

The pins fell, silently this time.

A boy appeared. Was it Cal?

Yes. Cal smiled at her. He lifted a bag. A green bowling bag.

"Is that yours?" Jenny asked.

Cal nodded with a grin. "Guess what's inside," he urged.

Jenny stared at the bowling bag. "What's inside?" she asked.

"Guess," Cal insisted stubbornly.

Jenny pulled the bag from Cal's hands. It wasn't as heavy as she'd imagined. In fact, it felt light, light as a feather.

"Guess what's inside," Cal repeated.

Jenny unzipped the bag. She pulled it open and peered inside.

A head stared up at her.

Claire's head.

Claire's head was in the bowling bag.

The head opened its eyes. Then its mouth twisted open, and it began to howl. A hideous animal howl.

Jenny held the bowling bag in both hands, and she began to howl, too. Jenny howled, and Claire's head howled.

Jenny awoke and sat straight up in bed.

The dream lingered. The howling didn't stop.

She pressed her hands against her ears. "What a weird dream!" she uttered.

But why didn't the howling stop?

Lowering her hands, she slowly realized the howls came from outside.

She lowered herself shakily to her feet. The strange cries seemed to come from nearby, from the backyard.

The ugly dream stayed with her as she made her way to the window. What on earth does it mean? she wondered, blinking hard, trying to force it to leave her mind.

And who is making those awful wails?

She pushed aside the curtains. Poked her head out the window.

Caught a glimpse of a blond-haired boy. Darting across the backyard.

"Sean? Is that you?" her sleep-choked voice didn't carry far. "Sean? Seth?"

The howls faded. The boy vanished.

Jenny stared down at the backyard, shivering.

*What is going on? What is happening?*

Half-awake, half in her dream, she stared out into the now-silent night, wondering what was real — and what wasn't.

She pulled herself up when she heard the sound behind her.

A floorboard creak. A footstep.

Someone is in my bedroom, Jenny realized.

# Chapter 17

Shivering, Jenny spun around.

Someone moved by the doorway.

The curtains wrapped around Jenny, tangled over her, clouding her view. With a low cry, she frantically pulled them away.

"Mom!" she whispered.

Mrs. Jeffers moved quickly toward Jenny. The moonlight revealed her worried expression. "What's wrong? I heard you walking around in here."

"I . . . uh . . . heard something," Jenny replied. She pointed to the window.

"Me, too," Mrs. Jeffers said softly.

Jenny let out a long sigh of relief. I didn't imagine it, she thought happily. Even Mom, who can sleep through anything, heard the howls, too.

"There's been a prowler in the neighborhood," her mom reported. "I didn't tell you. I didn't want to worry you. I mean — "

Jenny moved away from the window. "A prowler?"

"He doesn't steal anything," Mrs. Jeffers said. "He just does mischief. You know. Vandalism. He tips over garbage cans. Breaks windows. Cuts up lawn furniture. It happened at the Miller house two nights ago. They found their mailbox at the bottom of their swimming pool."

"Weird," Jenny commented. She dropped down onto the edge of the bed.

Mrs. Jeffers jammed her hands into the pockets of her bathrobe. She looked older to Jenny in the silvery light. The lines around her eyes seemed deeper. Her skin appeared pale and dry.

"I thought I saw a boy," Jenny said hesitantly.

"Huh? A boy?"

"Yeah. Running across the backyard," Jenny told her. "He had blond hair. Like . . . like next door."

Mrs. Jeffers chewed her bottom lip. "Maybe we should call the police."

Jenny shrugged. "It's quiet out there now."

Her mother crossed to the window and peered down. A few seconds later, she turned back into the room. "Such bright moonlight," she murmured. "I don't see anyone. Let's get back to sleep, okay?"

Jenny nodded. She slid under the covers.

Mrs. Jeffers bent over her, kissed her on the forehead, the way she did when Jenny was a little girl. "Sweet dreams."

"Good night, Mom," Jenny whispered.

As she shut her eyes, she pictured the sad-eyed girl in the attic window. Then the blond-haired boy racing across the backyard.

Something strange at the Warsaws', Jenny thought sleepily.

Something strange next door . . .

Her last thought before falling back to sleep.

Jenny pulled open the dishwasher door. "I'll take care of the dishes, Mom," she said. "I know you're in a hurry."

Mrs. Jeffers had a date with Winston. She carried two plates to the counter, a fretful expression on her face. "I'm forty-three years old," she moaned. "I shouldn't be worrying about what to wear on a date."

Jenny laughed. "It's good for you. You seem so much happier, Mom."

Mrs. Jeffers shook her head. "Happy? I'm not sure. Nervous? Definitely." She picked up the dish towel and started to wipe at a stain near the sink.

"Mom — go get dressed. I'll take care of it," Jenny insisted.

Mrs. Jeffers turned and headed out of the kitchen. "Are you seeing Cal tonight?" she called back.

"No," Jenny told her. "He's working the late shift at the garage."

"I have to get gas in my car," Mrs. Jeffers said. "I'll tell him you say hi."

Ten minutes later, Jenny's mom was dressed and out the door. Watching her speed away, Jenny had to smile. Her mom certainly had been acting like a lovesick teenager.

Jenny had just finished loading the dishwasher and wiping the counter clean when she heard a knock at the kitchen door. She turned as Mrs. Warsaw stepped into the room.

"Jenny — are you busy?" she asked breathlessly. Her face was flushed. She had beads of sweat on her wide forehead.

Jenny hesitated. "Busy?"

"Can you come stay with the kids? Just for a few hours?"

"Well . . ." Jenny started. "I don't — "

"My sister was taken ill," Mrs. Warsaw interrupted. "They took her to County General. They don't really know what's wrong. I know this is short notice. But I'm really worried about her. I can't take the kids with me, so . . ." Her voice trailed off. Her eyes pleaded with Jenny.

"Of course I'll stay with them," Jenny replied. "I'm not doing anything tonight."

"Oh, thank you! Thank you!" Mrs. Warsaw gushed. "You're a doll. You really are."

"I'll just grab my keys and come back with you," Jenny said.

"This is so nice of you," Mrs. Warsaw said, wiping her forehead with a chubby hand. "I'll pay you double, Jenny. I really will."

"That isn't necessary," Jenny called from the front hallway.

"My poor sister. She doesn't get a break," Mrs. Warsaw continued. "First Al died. Then, Clarice got sick. Now this."

Mrs. Warsaw kept talking, but Jenny couldn't hear her. She pulled her house keys from the bowl on the hall table. Then she checked herself out in the mirror on the wall by the front door.

Her hair was a total mess. She had put it up to keep it off her shoulders, and half of it had come loose. But she guessed it really didn't matter.

Poor Mrs. Warsaw, Jenny thought. She seems to be in such a panic.

I have to help her out, Jenny told herself. I really have no choice. I have to put my fears aside. At least for tonight. It's an emergency, after all.

I'm sure everything will be fine tonight, Jenny assured herself. Perfectly fine.

Sean and Meredith were playing a video game in the living room. Jenny greeted them warmly. They grunted hello, but didn't turn away from the fighting figures on the TV screen.

Mrs. Warsaw was nearly out the front door when she dropped her purse. The contents clattered to the floor, coins rolling away, a lipstick tube bouncing under the couch.

Jenny helped the frazzled woman stuff everything back in the bag. "I hope your sister is okay," she said. "Don't worry about the kids. We'll be fine here."

"I gave them dinner," Mrs. Warsaw replied, searching for her car keys. "But they may want dessert later. There's a cake in a box on the counter. Be sure to help yourself, Jenny."

Mrs. Warsaw pushed open the screen door. "Be good, kids," she called back to them. "No fighting." She disappeared out the door.

Sean and Meredith didn't turn around.

"Die! Die, you scum!" Sean was screaming, frantically working the control pad.

"Where's Seth?" Jenny asked, dropping down onto the couch.

They didn't reply.

She was about to go searching for him when he walked into the room. He was wearing a sleeveless blue T-shirt and baggy blue shorts. "Hi, Jenny." He smiled at her. "I *thought* I heard you come in."

"Your mom had to go visit her sister," Jenny reported.

"I know," he replied, glancing at the noisy battle on the TV screen. "Hey, I get to play next!"

"When can we have cake?" Meredith demanded. Her first words to Jenny that evening.

"Yeah. We want cake!" Sean repeated.

All three began to chant: "We want cake! We want cake!"

"Okay, okay." Jenny jumped to her feet. "I'll go get it. But you'll have to come in the kitchen. You can't eat it in the living room."

Wow, she thought. Am I starting to sound like a parent or what?

Jenny found the white cake box on the kitchen counter. She cut the string with a pair of scissors, opened the lid, and carefully pulled out the cake.

"Mmmmm." She scooped a glob of chocolate frosting onto her finger and tasted it. Not bad. Maybe I'll have a slice, too, she decided.

She found a large cake knife in a wooden knife rack beside the toaster oven. Then she pulled down four small plates from the cabinet.

She was raising the heavy knife to slice the cake when she felt the sudden pressure on her arm.

"Hey — !" she cried out, startled.

She struggled to lower the knife. But something was pushing it, pushing it with great force. Something pushed her hand, pushed the knife away from the cake.

"Hey! What on earth — !"

Jenny struggled. But the invisible force overpowered her.

The wide blade gleamed in the bright kitchen light.

The knife turned in her hand.

"No!" she cried, trying to push the knife away, trying to get control of it.

The blade edged closer.

"No!"

She wasn't strong enough. Wasn't as strong as the invisible force.

She uttered a desperate cry.

And the blade plunged into her chest.

# Chapter 18

"Noooo!"

Jenny stumbled back as the knife shot forward.

As the blade point started to pierce the front of her T-shirt, she dropped to the floor.

She landed hard. Pain shot up through her body.

She saw the knife sail over her shoulder, heard it clatter to the floor behind her.

She grabbed her chest.

*I'm okay. I'm okay.*

Breathing hard, her heart thumping, she pulled herself to a sitting position. She rubbed the front of her T-shirt, rubbed it until she was sure she wasn't cut.

And then she stared down at the knife.

"How — ?" she murmured out loud.

She turned to see the three kids in the

kitchen doorway, staring down at her in horror.

"Oh. Uh . . ." Had they seen the whole thing?

Had they seen her strange tug-of-war? Had they seen her nearly stab herself to death?

Seth was the first to move. "Jenny — what happened? Did you fall?" He came running over to help pull her to her feet.

Jenny sucked in a deep breath, tried to steady her trembling legs. They didn't see it, she decided. I can't tell them what happened. I don't want to frighten them.

*And I don't want them to think I'm crazy.*

"I — I slipped," she stammered. She leaned against the counter.

She turned to Sean, still in the doorway. He had a faint smile on his face. "Did you cut yourself?" he asked.

Jenny shook her head. "No. The knife just fell. I'm all right." She rubbed the front of her T-shirt, making sure one more time.

Why is Sean smiling like that? she wondered.

Seth carefully picked up the knife and handed it to her.

"Can we have our cake now?" Meredith demanded impatiently.

"Coming right up," Jenny replied, forcing a smile.

The kids enjoyed their cake. Meredith asked for seconds. The two boys hurried back to their video battle in front of the TV set.

Jenny felt too shaken to have a slice. She rinsed the cake knife off and examined it.

Nothing unusual.

A chill ran down her back. She felt confused and frightened. But she had to carry on, had to pretend that everything was okay. She didn't want to worry the kids.

The sink was piled high with dirty dishes from dinner. I'll load them in the dishwasher after I get the kids to bed, Jenny decided.

A short while later, Sean and Meredith got into a fight. Jenny wasn't even sure what it was about. She glanced up to see them wrestling on the living room carpet, screaming and flailing at each other.

She pulled them apart and took Meredith to bed. But Meredith was not in a cooperative mood. Jenny had to read her two Roald Dahl stories before she agreed to go to sleep.

When she finally returned to the living room, Jenny found the two boys watching a very adult movie on one of the cable movie channels.

After a ten-minute argument about why she couldn't allow them to watch that movie, she got them to agree to watching a tape. That led to another long argument about what tape to watch.

It was nearly eleven when she finally tucked the two boys into bed. She turned out their light and made her way down the hall.

She stopped at the attic door.

The face of the sad-eyed girl floated into her memory.

Jenny pressed her ear against the door and listened. Silence.

She tried the doorknob. It turned easily. But the door wouldn't pull open. It was locked.

She returned to the living room, feeling uneasy, wondering how late Mrs. Warsaw would be. She glanced at the clock on the mantel. Too late to call Claire.

Jenny swallowed hard. It would be nice to have some company, she thought. Cal was still at work. Her mother wasn't home yet.

She stepped into the kitchen and carried the dirty cake plates to the sink. Then she pulled open the dishwasher. I'll be better off if I keep busy, she told herself. She began rinsing off the dinner dishes and loading them into the dishwasher.

The job took only a few minutes. When the

dishes were all loaded, Jenny saw that the sink was filled with melon rinds and food scraps.

She shoved them into the drain. Found the switch for the garbage disposal and clicked it on.

It started up with a roar.

Water from the faucet flowed into the drain. The disposal made a deafening grinding sound as it began to devour the food scraps.

Jenny slid some more scraps toward the drain.

Then she felt the pressure on her hand.

Like an invisible hand, gripping hers, pushing it forward.

Pushing her hand toward the roaring drain. Pushing her. Pushing her.

"*No — !*"

Jenny pushed back. Tried to leap back from the sink.

But the invisible force held her in place.

"*Please — !*" she screamed.

Straining, struggling, pulling back with all of her might, she watched her hand being forced into the grinding disposal blades.

Closer. Closer. The hot water spilling over the back of her hand. Her fingers disappearing into the drain now.

"*Oh, please — !*"

And then, in her terror, in her desperate

panic — a moment of clear thought.

With a frantic cry, she reached up her free hand — and clicked off the disposal.

The blades whirred to a stop. The roar faded to silence.

The invisible force vanished at once, leaving Jenny sobbing, leaning over the sink, her entire body trembling.

She sucked in breath after breath, trying to stop the shaking, the cold chills, the sobs from deep in her throat.

After a few seconds, she sensed that she wasn't alone.

She could feel someone close by, someone behind her.

Taking a deep breath, she spun around.

"Sean!" she choked out.

He stood inches away from her. His brown eyes stared up at her from under his tousled blond hair.

How long has he been standing here? Jenny wondered.

"Jenny — " he whispered, his eyes urgently locked on hers. "Jenny, I have to tell you something. Something very scary."

# Chapter 19

"Huh?" Jenny stared down at him, struggling to think clearly. "Sean — what is it? What's the matter? Did you — ?"

"Jenny, please listen — " Sean urged in a whisper. He grabbed her arm. His hand felt so cold.

"What, Sean?" Jenny whispered back.

They both turned to the doorway as Seth strode into the room. "Can I have a glass of water?" he demanded. His eyes were on his twin brother.

Sean let go of Jenny's arm. He took a step back, his expression tight with fear.

"In a second," Jenny told Seth. She turned back to Sean. "What did you want to tell me, Sean? Go ahead. What is it?"

Sean hesitated. "Uh . . . I want water, too." He darted a glance at his brother.

Seth grinned at him.

"But you said — " Jenny started.

Sean shook his head. She saw his chin quiver. She could still see fear in his eyes. "No. Just water," Sean insisted. "I just came down for water."

"So Mrs. W got home after midnight?" Claire asked. She sat up and pulled a bottle of suntan lotion from her bag.

"Uh-huh," Jenny replied sleepily. "I was up almost all night. I couldn't get to sleep."

Claire rubbed a glob of the white lotion on her shoulders. Then she reached behind her and adjusted the back of her blue bikini top. "Want some?" She pushed the lotion bottle toward Jenny.

"No thanks." Jenny pushed her sunglasses up on her nose. "I want to burn for a while. The sun feels so good."

They had spread a blanket on the grassy lakeshore and were stretched out in their swimsuits, sunning and talking quietly. It was the next afternoon, a sultry, hot Saturday. The sun beamed down in a bright, cloudless sky. There was no wind at all. Not a leaf trembled on the trees behind the lakeshore.

Jenny needed to relax. And she needed to confide in someone.

What had happened at Mrs. Warsaw's house

was just too frightening. Jenny made Claire promise not to tell a soul. Then she told Claire the entire story.

Claire listened in silence, her dark eyes narrowed on the lake, her expression thoughtful.

Jenny told her about the girl in the window. About the strange howls at night. The blond boy running through the backyard. The whispered threats at Mrs. Warsaw's house. The cake knife. The garbage disposal.

When she finished, she waited for Claire to react.

But Claire stared back at her in silence for the longest time. Finally, she said softly, "Jenny, have you told this to Dr. Simonson?"

Jenny sat up on the blanket and uttered an angry cry. "You think I'm imagining it all — don't you, Claire!" she snapped angrily.

Claire didn't reply.

"You think I'm cracking up again!" Jenny accused. "Poor crazy Jenny — she's seeing things again. Is that what you think, Claire? Is it?" Jenny shrieked.

"Shhhh. Calm down," Claire replied softly. "I — I don't know what to think," she confessed. "I mean, the whole story — it's so . . . so . . ."

"So *crazy*?" Jenny finished the sentence for her.

"Come on, Jen — give me a break," Claire pleaded. "I'm trying to understand. But flying knives? Invisible hands shoving you into the disposal?"

"It happened!" Jenny insisted heatedly. "I didn't imagine it. It happened." Jenny uttered a sob. "You're my best friend, Claire. I thought that *you* would believe me."

"Okay, okay. I'm trying," Claire replied. "But you have to tell your psychiatrist, Jen. You have to tell her that — "

"I can't!" Jenny protested. "Don't you understand? She'll send me back to the hospital. But I'm not crazy. I'm not!"

Jenny grabbed Claire by the shoulders. Her hands slid over the greasy suntan oil. "You won't tell — will you? You won't tell anyone? You promised!"

Claire's eyes burned into Jenny's. "But what are you going to *do*?" she demanded.

"I'm going to prove that I'm not crazy," Jenny told her. "I'm going to prove that it all really happened. And I'm going to find out why."

When the howls rose up from the backyard late that night, Jenny was ready. She had stayed dressed. Had dozed in the chair beside her bedroom window.

The low animal wails made her jump to her feet, instantly alert. She leaned on the windowsill and peered down.

Into hazy swirls of fog.

Hot air fluttered her hair. She realized she was sweating.

The night felt as hot and humid as the day. A fog had descended around dinnertime, damp and gray. Now the moonlight shimmered off the fog clouds, making the backyard appear eerie. Unfamiliar.

Another howl rose up from the yard. And Jenny caught a glimpse of the little, blond-haired boy, dancing through the fog.

She spun away from the window, her heart pounding, and crept out of her room. Down the stairs, as silently as she could. And out the backdoor.

The fog billowed around her, damp and warm. She could feel the moisture on her skin as she stepped into the yard, her eyes adjusting to the moonlight.

Shadows flickered and tossed beneath the fog swirls. The trees rose up at the back of the yard like dark giants. A curtain of fog fell between the two yards, hiding the fence that separated Jenny's house from Mrs. Warsaw's.

Jenny heard another howl, distant now. She

turned, trying to figure out its direction. Eager to follow it.

She heard laughter, a high, boyish giggle. Cold laughter. Cruel.

"Sean — is that you?" she called. "Sean?" Silence.

The dark trees shivered in a hot gust of wind. Shadows bent and tossed.

What am I doing out here? she asked herself.

*Solving the mystery,* came the answer.

*Solving the mystery so no one can accuse you of being crazy.*

*Solving the mystery so you never have to return to that hospital.*

Another shrill laugh. Right behind her?

She whirled around. Stared into the fog. Saw only flickering shadows.

"Sean? Are you out here? Answer me — please!"

The next giggle made her jump. So close. So close it could be coming from her own mouth. Inside her own head.

No!

No, I'm *not* imagining it!

No. It's real. It's real laughter.

The blood pounded at her temples. Despite the heat, Jenny felt chills.

She took a step toward the Warsaws' yard. Then another.

"Sean? Are you laughing? Are you out here?"

And then Jenny uttered a startled gasp as she heard thudding footsteps.

She felt hot breath on the back of her neck — as two strong hands shoved her hard from behind.

# Chapter 20

Jenny landed hard on her elbows and knees.

With a frightened cry, she spun around and stared up at the enormous creature, panting excitedly beside her.

"Killer!" she cried hoarsely. "What are you doing out here?"

The big German shepherd wagged his shaggy tail at the sound of his name. His sides moved in and out like bellows, and his tongue hung out between his jagged teeth.

"You're hot, huh?" Jenny asked, climbing to her knees.

The dog lumbered forward and licked Jenny's face, nearly toppling her over again.

"Killer, you scared me to death," Jenny told the dog, scratching his collar. She shoved him away gently and pulled herself to her feet. "Are you being a good watchdog?"

The dog panted loudly in reply.

"Did you see a boy out here, Killer?" Jenny demanded, letting her eyes wander around the yard.

She pushed her hair back off her face. It felt so wet. She wiped the sweat off her forehead with the back of one hand.

Killer lumbered toward the fence, sniffing the ground, his tail straight up behind him. She watched him until he disappeared behind the curtain of fog.

Jenny turned back toward her house.

I've lost him, she thought, disappointed. No sign of the blond-haired boy. Whoever it was, he's gone now.

And then she heard the shrill laughter, so close, so close to her . . . so cold and ugly.

"Who's there?" Jenny cried. "Who?"

No one there.

"Jenny?" a familiar voice shouted. "Jenny? Come here!"

Her mother called to her from the back-door.

The kitchen light flashed on as Jenny made her way into the house. Mrs. Jeffers stood in her bathrobe, her face lined with worry, her eyes still half-closed with sleep, her hands pressed tightly at her waist.

"Mom, I . . . uh . . ." Jenny started.

"What on earth?" Mrs. Jeffers exclaimed.

"What were you doing out there, Jen? It's nearly two in the morning."

"Well . . ." Jenny took a deep breath. She swallowed hard, tried to slow her pounding heart.

"Look at you!" her mother cried. "You're soaked! You're dripping wet. What were you doing out there?"

Jenny pushed back her hair again. She suddenly felt weak. Exhausted. "I heard those howls again," she told her mother. "I saw a boy. A blond boy. I thought it was — "

"You got dressed and chased after him?" Mrs. Jeffers demanded.

"I — I stayed dressed," Jenny confessed. "I had to find out — "

Mrs. Jeffers' jaw twitched. "We'll have to have a talk in the morning," she said softly. "A serious talk, Jen." She let out a long sigh.

"But, Mom — "

"I can't let you baby-sit next door anymore," her mother continued, tensely shoving her hands into the robe pockets. "It hasn't been good for you. These things you're seeing. These voices and things — "

Jenny let out a shriek. "Claire *told* you?" she cried.

Mrs. Jeffers nodded grimly. "She called me this afternoon. She told me . . . about you."

Jenny balled her hands into tight fists. "She *promised* me! She promised me she wouldn't tell!" she raged.

"Jen — she's your friend. She's worried about you," Mrs. Jeffers replied softly, her jaw clenching and unclenching again. "She did what she thought was best for you."

Jenny paced furiously back and forth. "I can't *believe* she called you!" she cried. She glared angrily at her mother. "Does *everyone* around here think I'm totally Looney Tunes? Even my best friend?"

"No one thinks you're sick again," Mrs. Jeffers replied, speaking carefully. "But you know yourself that you're supposed to avoid strain. You're not supposed to stress yourself out." She sighed. "We'll call Dr. Simonson in the morning. I'm sure that she will want to talk — "

Jenny stopped pacing. She locked her eyes on her mother. "Mom, I'm going back to Mrs. Warsaw's," she said firmly. "I don't care what you say. I'm not crazy. I'm not imagining anything."

"Jen — it's late," her mother started. "And you've gotten yourself worked up into a state. In the morning — "

"Mom, Mrs. Warsaw needs me," Jenny insisted, speaking slowly, softly. "I'm going back

there to baby-sit. One more time. One more
time, Mom. And I'm going to find out what's
going on over there. So that no one can call
me crazy again."

"Jenny, you look tired," Mrs. Warsaw said.
She stood in her kitchen, loading plastic con-
tainers of food into two large brown shopping
bags.

Jenny sighed. "I didn't get much sleep last
night." She picked up a container labeled SOUP
and handed it to Mrs. Warsaw.

"I kept hearing the strangest howls all
night," Jenny continued. "Out in back. Did you
hear them, too?"

Mrs. Warsaw shook her head. Her tight
ringlets bounced around her face. "I'm a very
heavy sleeper," she replied. "The house could
fall in, and I wouldn't hear it."

Jenny had hurried over after dinner. Her
mother tried to convince her not to baby-sit.
"I'll go in your place," Mrs. Jeffers offered.

"I'll be okay, Mom," Jenny assured her.
"Mrs. Warsaw said she's only staying at her
sister's for a short while." Jenny had forced a
smile. She squeezed her mother's hand. "Besides, you're right next door. What can happen?"

Now she helped Mrs. Warsaw load the food

bags into the backseat of her car. "Where are the kids?" she asked.

Mrs. Warsaw brushed a mosquito off her chubby arm. "Upstairs. In Sean's room, I think. They were playing a board game last time I checked."

Jenny followed Mrs. Warsaw back to the house. The sun was setting behind the trees. A white half-moon hovered low in the graying sky.

Mrs. Warsaw pulled her car keys from her bag. She hoisted the bag on her shoulder and headed out the door. "Don't let Meredith stay up too late," she instructed. "She looked a little pale to me today."

Jenny nodded. "No problem." The screen door slammed behind Mrs. Warsaw. Jenny glanced quickly around the kitchen.

Her eyes stopped at the sink. She felt a chill as she remembered the grinding roar of the garbage disposal, the powerful, invisible force that pushed her hand into the drain.

Swallowing hard, she forced herself to turn away from the sink. Her heart pounding, she ran from the kitchen.

She found the three kids in the twins' room. They were seated on the floor around a game board. Cards and dice and scorecards were scattered around the board.

Both boys were barefoot. They both wore baggy blue shorts without shirts.

They're both so pale and skinny, Jenny thought. I can practically see their ribs.

Meredith was already dressed for bed, in an enormous white T-shirt that came down to her ankles.

"Hey, guys — what's up?" Jenny called cheerfully.

"We're playing Clue," Sean told her.

Meredith frowned up at Jenny. "I don't really *get* this game."

"It's kind of a hard game for you," Jenny replied.

"I'm helping her," Seth said.

Jenny lowered herself to the carpet and watched the game. The culprit turned out to be Colonel Mustard in the library with the candlestick.

Seth was the first to figure it out. Meredith shook her head unhappily. "How did you *do* that?" she asked her brother. "I still don't get it."

Jenny started to relax. The kids seemed to be in very good moods, less tense than usual. She joined in the next game. They played quietly, without any arguing at all.

After a second game, Jenny tucked

Meredith into bed. Then she helped the boys put the game away.

Seth kept staring at her, she noticed. He seemed to be watching her, studying her.

She followed them downstairs. They wanted to watch TV.

But Jenny decided she had to ask them some questions.

She made them sit side by side on the living room couch. Then she stood in front of them, her arms crossed over her chest.

"Did we do something wrong?" Sean asked innocently.

"I just want to ask you about something," Jenny replied. She paused, thinking hard, trying to decide where to begin.

The boys exchanged glances. Sean scratched his bare chest.

"Last night, I heard strange noises outside," Jenny began. "And I looked out my window and saw a boy running across the backyard."

She turned to Sean. "Was that *you* running outside after midnight last night?"

Sean's eyes widened. He glanced again at his brother. When he turned back to Jenny, he had a fretful expression on his face.

"Yes," he said softly, so softly Jenny could barely hear him. "It was me."

# Chapter 21

Her arms still crossed tightly in front of her, Jenny stared down at Sean. She hadn't expected him to confess.

A grin spread over Seth's face. He giggled and poked Sean hard with his elbow.

Sean's solemn expression cracked, and he started to giggle, too. The boys slapped each other high fives.

Jenny stared at them in confusion. "You mean — ?" she stated.

"You're such a jerk!" Seth told his brother. They both giggled some more.

"It wasn't Sean. It was me!" Seth declared, laughing.

"Liar!" Sean cried, shoving his brother. "It was me! I go out every night and howl at the moon!"

They both tossed back their heads and started to howl at the top of their lungs.

"Ssshhh! Quiet! Stop it!" Jenny demanded angrily. "Meredith is trying to sleep — remember?"

Sean and Seth continued to giggle, very pleased with themselves.

"Ha-ha," Jenny said sarcastically. "You guys are a riot." She sighed angrily. "You didn't have to lie to me. I asked you a serious question."

Their grins faded. "Did you really see a boy in the backyard?" Seth demanded.

"Yes," Jenny replied quickly. "I mean . . . I'm *pretty* sure. I know I heard him laughing. And . . . and . . ."

"It was very foggy last night," Seth said.

"How do *you* know?" Jenny asked suspiciously.

"I woke up. I was very thirsty. I looked out my window. It was really creepy out. Kind of scary-looking."

For some reason, Seth's explanation made Sean laugh and shake his head.

Seth flashed his brother an angry glance, and Sean cut his laughter short.

"Can we make popcorn?" Sean asked.

Jenny raised her eyes to the mantel clock. "It's kind of late."

"We'll go to bed right after popcorn," Sean promised.

Jenny reluctantly agreed. She headed to the kitchen, thinking about what had just happened. The boys had treated my question about last night as a total joke, she realized. They didn't take me seriously for a moment.

But I did see a blond-haired boy running through the fog last night.

And if it wasn't Sean or Seth — who was it?

They didn't go to bed after popcorn, as promised. They begged to watch TV. When there wasn't anything on that they liked, they begged to play just one Super-Nintendo game.

Which turned into *two* games.

It was nearly eleven when Jenny finally tucked them into bed. She said good night, turned down their second requests for a glass of water, and returned to the living room.

She gazed uncertainly around the room. She picked up the game cartridges and stacked them beside the TV. Then she started to pace nervously back and forth.

So far, the evening had been peaceful. Even relaxing.

But Jenny knew that when the kids were tucked in their beds . . .

When the kids were tucked in and the house fell quiet . . .

That's when the eerie chill descended over the room. That's when the frightening whispers came.

As they did tonight.

As they did again tonight.

The horrifying, whispered threat. So close . . . so close to Jenny's ear.

The same tonight. But different. Much different.

*"Jenny, you saw me."*

She stopped pacing. Whirled around. Felt the sudden whiff of frigid air.

Her eyes swept the room.

But of course she saw no one.

"Who are you? What do you want?" she choked out.

*"Jenny, you saw me last night,"* the voice repeated. So close. As if whispering in her ear. *"Now you have to die. Now you have to die TONIGHT!"*

# Chapter 22

Jenny uttered a gasp as the cold swirled around her.

She felt the clammy touch of bone-hard fingers against her cheek.

"Noooooo!" A terrified howl burst from her throat.

She pulled back, away from the cold, invisible touch.

Stumbled against the coffee table. Struggled to keep from falling backwards over it.

The icy fingers slid over the back of her neck.

"Nooooooo!"

She ducked away. Spun toward the stairs. Started to run.

A damp chill, a wave of cold swept over her, holding her, pushing her back.

She heard laughter, as cold as the air.

*"You die tonight, Jenny!"*

She opened her mouth to scream again. But the sound choked in her throat.

The chill air rolled over her, washed against her, wave after wave.

She ducked her head, shut her eyes, and dove through the cold.

The stairs rose in front of her.

The cruel laughter followed close behind as she plunged into the stairwell.

The stairs tilted and swayed.

She grasped the iron banister. Pulled herself up, step by step.

She felt the cold at her back. Heard the laughter rising behind her.

*Where can I go?* she asked herself. *Where can I hide?*

She stumbled at the landing. Hit her knee hard on the top step.

The cold swept over her. Pushed her back into the stairwell.

A choking, thick cold that took her breath away.

She sucked in a mouthful of air. It tasted sour.

Her eyes darted over the narrow hallway.

*Where to run? Where to hide?*

Into the bathroom across from the twins room.

She grabbed frantically for the door. Slammed it hard behind her.

Locked it with a trembling hand.

Stood in the dark for a long moment. Not breathing. Not moving.

Listening. Listening for the laughter. For the whispery voice.

Her heart thudding, making her chest ache. Flashing streaks of white light blazing in her eyes. She blinked. Blinked again.

Am I safe here in the darkness?

Have I shut the voice out? Have I shut the owner of the clammy fingers out in the hall?

Silence. Such a heavy silence.

She fumbled for the light switch. Clicked on the ceiling light. It flickered on.

So bright.

She waited for her eyes to adjust.

Listened. Listened.

Silence still.

Jenny raised her eyes to the medicine chest mirror.

She gasped when she saw the reflection.

A face stared back at her.

Not her face.

Sean's face.

# Chapter 23

Jenny uttered a startled cry.

She spun around. "How — how did you get in here?" she stammered.

No one there.

Her eyes bulged in disbelief.

She turned back to the mirror.

He smiled out at her in the glass.

She spun back toward the door.

Not there.

No one there but her.

She stood alone in the tiny bathroom.

"Noooo!" A moan of horror burst from her lips.

The pale face grinned gleefully at her from the mirror.

"Are you — are you Sean?" she choked out.

The face in the mirror shook his head no. His grin didn't fade. His eyes gleamed with pleasure.

"You're *Seth*?" Jenny demanded.

His grin widened as he nodded yes.

"Oh." Her entire body convulsed in a tremor of shock.

"Seth — where are you? Seth?"

Jenny spun around again.

Not there. Not standing behind her.

She pulled back the shower curtain.

Not hiding in the tub.

Not in the room. Not there.

But grinning out at her from the mirror.

"Seth — please — " she started.

His grin faded quickly. His eyes narrowed cruelly. His expression hardened until Jenny barely recognized him.

"*Jenny — you die TONIGHT!*" Seth whispered from the mirror.

# Chapter 24

The cold rose up from the bathroom floor.

In the mirror, Seth's leering face began to glow. Brighter. Brighter. Until his whole head gleamed like gold.

*"Jenny — you die TONIGHT!"*

"It was you!" Jenny shrieked in a shrill voice that tore out of her throbbing chest. "Seth — it was you! But — why?"

*"The baby-sitter has to die!"* the glowing reflection cried.

"No!" Jenny shrieked. "No!"

The boy's face sneered at her from inside the glass.

"No! No!" She chanted without hearing herself.

With a gasp of terror, of anger, of panic, she grabbed up the heavy china flower vase that rested beside the sink.

Tilted the dried flowers out onto the vanity counter.

Pulled back her arm.

And let out a defiant cry as she heaved the vase at the leering face in the mirror.

The face appeared to crack as the mirror shattered.

Jenny gaped in horror, watching the vase tumble to the floor. Watching the face in the mirror appear to split apart.

Sections of mirror fell away.

Then the whole mirror toppled out of its frame.

Shards of glass flew.

Jenny reached out to shield herself.

And a jagged piece of mirror scraped over her open hand.

She didn't feel it at first.

Then a line of pain shot up her arm. And she stared in surprise as the bright red blood spurted up from the deep cut in her hand and flowed over her wrist.

"Ohhh." She grabbed at her wrist. Watched the blood smear over her other hand.

Watched it drip, drip, drip to the floor. A bright red rivulet, so warm.

"Jenny — ?"

A voice behind her.

Someone else in the room.

"Jenny — ?"

Holding her throbbing hand, feeling the warm blood flow down her arm, Jenny turned.

"Mrs. Warsaw!"

The woman filled the doorway, her mouth open in shock, her eyes lowered to the flowing, dripping blood. "Jenny — what have you done?" she cried. "How — ?"

"I — I — " Jenny sputtered. She raised her hand to point to the medicine chest, and the blood dripped down the front of her T-shirt.

"What have you done?" Mrs. Warsaw murmured again. She slid past Jenny, into the room, careful to step around the widening puddle of blood on the white tile floor.

"I — I — " Jenny still couldn't find the words.

Mrs. Warsaw frantically began pulling up tissues from the dispenser on the counter. Broken glass crunched beneath her shoes.

She jammed a thick wad of tissues against the cut on Jenny's hand. "Let's get you home. Quick. Let's get you home."

"Th-thank you," Jenny finally managed to say. The words sounded odd. Out of place. Meaningless. She didn't know what else to say.

They started out the door. Jenny glanced down at the trail of blood she was leaving.

"Wait." Mrs. Warsaw stopped, turned. She grabbed a green bath towel off the rack. She wrapped it tightly around Jenny's wrist. "Hold it. Hold it in place," she instructed. "We've got to stop that bleeding."

Jenny nodded. She struggled to hold the towel in place. Her legs felt rubbery and weak as she followed Mrs. Warsaw into the hall.

Down the stairs.

Jenny let out a moan of pain. Mrs. Warsaw wrapped a heavy arm around her waist and guided her out the backdoor. Into a warm, starless night.

"How did you do that?" Mrs. Warsaw murmured as they hurried toward Jenny's house. "How did you ever do it?"

Jenny's mom appeared at the backdoor. The light came on. Then Jenny saw her mother running barefoot across the yard, running to meet them.

"What happened? What happened?" Mrs. Jeffers cried. She gasped as she drew closer. "Oh! So much blood!"

"We've got to get a doctor," Mrs. Warsaw urged. "We've got to stop the bleeding."

"Just a cut," Jenny managed to tell her mother. "Not as bad as it looks. Really."

"But what happened?" Mrs. Jeffers demanded, helping guide Jenny into the house.

"The mirror broke," Mrs. Warsaw told her. "Glass all over."

"The twins," Jenny murmured, trying to clear her head, trying to explain to them.

"What?" Mrs. Warsaw's face filled with confusion.

"Sean and Seth," Jenny said. "I saw Seth in the yard at night. And then in the mirror, and — "

"Who?" Mrs. Warsaw demanded.

Mrs. Jeffers stared at Jenny, her features tight with concern.

"Your twins," Jenny repeated. "I knew there was something strange about the twins. But — I just couldn't figure it out. Until . . . until . . ."

"Oh, child!" Mrs. Warsaw sighed, her eyes brimming with tears. "Oh, child. Oh, child."

"Something strange about the twins," Jenny insisted.

Mrs. Warsaw placed a tender hand on Jenny's trembling shoulder. "Oh, child," she repeated. "Oh, Jenny. You poor thing. I don't *have* twins!"

# Chapter 25

Jenny stared down at her bandaged hand. It made her think of mummies.

That's what I'll be, she thought glumly, letting a tear roll down her cheek. That's what I'll be if I have to go back to the hospital. A mummy. Locked tightly away.

A loud sob escaped her throat. But she forced back the tears that threatened to fall.

Her mother had cleaned the cut and carefully bandaged it. It hadn't been as deep as it seemed. It wouldn't require stitches.

Mrs. Jeffers took Jenny up to her bedroom and told her to lie down and rest. A few seconds later, Jenny overheard her mother on the phone. She had called Dr. Simonson. She was leaving a message about Jenny on her answering machine.

Mom thinks I'm crazy, Jenny told herself.

I *am* crazy!

*No twins. No twins.*

The words repeated in her mind like a sorrowful chant.

Mrs. Warsaw doesn't have twins. She only has Sean and Meredith.

That means I imagined Seth, Jenny told herself. That means I imagined a boy who looks just like Sean.

But — wait.

Sean talked to Seth, too.

And Meredith talked to Seth.

Both kids played ball with Seth. Seth and Sean played video games together all the time.

So how could I have made him up? Jenny asked herself. How could Seth exist only in my mind?

She shut her eyes and pressed both hands against her throbbing temples. So confused . . . I'm so totally confused.

She could hear her mother down in the kitchen, talking to Mrs. Warsaw.

They're talking about me, Jenny knew. They're talking about how crazy I am, how I saw a boy that doesn't exist.

Jenny climbed to her feet. She crept out of the room, to the stairway. She stopped halfway down, listening to the conversation in the kitchen.

"The doctor will know what's best," Mrs.

Jeffers was saying. "I just can't believe it's
. . . happening to Jenny again."

Mrs. Warsaw muttered a reply. Jenny
couldn't hear it.

Jenny sat down on the step and rested her
head against the wooden banister.

After a few seconds, she heard Mrs.
Warsaw continue. "We almost didn't buy the
house. You know. Because of the stories."

"Stories?" Jenny heard her mother ask.

"About the boy," Mrs. Warsaw explained.
"The boy who was murdered in the house. By
his baby-sitter. When the real estate agent told
us, I wasn't sure I wanted to live here."

A long silence.

Jenny lifted her head. Listened hard, her
mind spinning.

"Oh, how horrible!" her mother exclaimed
to Mrs. Warsaw. "Maybe Jenny heard the
story about the murdered boy. Maybe it
stayed buried in her mind somehow. And
when she started going to your house to baby-
sit . . ."

"The boy came to life in Jenny's mind," Mrs.
Warsaw finished the sentence for Jenny's
mother.

"No!" Jenny murmured out loud. "No. I
didn't imagine Seth. I'm not crazy! I'm not!"

"I'm taking Sean and Meredith to my sister's," she heard Mrs. Warsaw announce.

"When?" Mrs. Jeffers asked.

"Right now. I want to spend the night with my sister. I might stay for a day or two." A pause. And then Mrs. Warsaw added, "I hope everything is all right. With Jenny."

"I hope so, too," Jenny's mother replied uncertainly.

I'm *not* crazy! Jenny thought, jumping to her feet. I'm *not* going back to the hospital! Never!

She heard the backdoor slam. Heard her mother making her way to the stairs. Jenny turned and ran back to her room.

She sat down in the dark on the edge of the bed. Then she stood up and started to pace, her arms crossed in front of her.

A boy was murdered, she thought. A boy was murdered in Mrs. Warsaw's house. Murdered by his baby-sitter.

"Jenny? Are you okay?" Mrs. Jeffers stepped into the room. "What are you doing?" She clicked on the ceiling light.

"Just thinking," Jenny replied.

Mrs. Jeffers crossed the room quickly and hugged Jenny. "You'll be okay. I know you will. Get undressed, okay? Get some sleep. Tomorrow morning we'll . . ." Her voice trailed off.

"We'll go see Dr. Simonson," Jenny finished the thought for her.

"That little boy you saw — " Mrs. Jeffers started.

"He was *there*, Mom!" Jenny cried heatedly. "You've got to believe me. I didn't make him up! He was there!"

Her mother sighed. "Please get some sleep, Jenny. I know you'll feel a lot better after we see the doctor."

For several minutes after her mother left the room, Jenny continued to pace back and forth, thinking hard, thinking about Seth, about how sweet he had seemed. And then she remembered his cruel, hard face in the bathroom mirror. His taunting laugh. His threats.

*"The baby-sitter has to die!"* Seth had said. So angrily. So bitterly.

I didn't make it up, Jenny told herself for the hundredth time. I didn't make Seth up.

She heard voices in the backyard. Peering out the window, she saw Mrs. Warsaw load the two kids into the backseat of her car. Sean and Meredith were in pajamas. Meredith clutched a small brown teddy bear.

A few seconds later, the headlights flashed on, and the car backed down the driveway and rolled off into the night.

Jenny sighed.

Two kids. Just two kids.

She started to turn away — but a movement in the upstairs window of the Warsaws' house caught her eye.

Something moved in the attic window next door.

Jenny squinted into the moonlight.

A face. A face in the attic window.

Jenny recognized it. The girl. The sad-eyed girl.

She was staring back at Jenny. And again her lips moved in the same silent plea: "Help me. Help me."

Am I imagining her, too? Jenny wondered. Is she only in my mind?

She had to find out.

"Help me," the girl pleaded, her face pressed against the glass. "Help me."

"Okay," Jenny said out loud. "I'll help you. I'm coming over there. Right now."

# Chapter 26

She paused at the bottom of the stairs, making sure her mother hadn't heard. Then she slipped out the front door, carefully closing the screen door behind her.

As she silently made her way around to the back, Jenny gazed up at the Warsaws' attic window. The moon had sunk behind heavy clouds. Darkness covered the window now.

I'm coming, Jenny thought, searching for the sad-eyed girl. I'm coming to let you out. Whoever you are.

She stumbled over Sean's bike in the driveway, but caught her balance. Her heart pounded as she stepped up to the Warsaws' backdoor.

So dark. Without the moon shining down, the house hovered in total blackness, like a dark, silent creature waiting to swallow her up.

Jenny tried the backdoor. It pushed open easily. In all the confusion, Mrs. Warsaw had left it unlocked. Taking a deep breath, Jenny slipped into the house.

Past the cluttered kitchen. The empty popcorn bowls from earlier that night still strewn on the counter. Mrs. Warsaw hadn't bothered to clean up. She must have been really eager to get back to her sister's, Jenny realized.

Her sneakers squeaked on the linoleum as she crossed the kitchen and made her way into the living room. Her heart thudded in her chest. Her skin began to tingle.

She climbed the stairs slowly, pulling herself up one step at a time. She listened hard, alert to every sound, every creak of the stairs, every sigh of the house.

She stopped at the second-floor landing. The hallway was too dark to see anything. The door to the attic was down at the other end.

Jenny fumbled along the wall. Found the light switcn. Clicked on the yellow ceiling light.

The narrow hall stretched before her. Silent. The air so hot and stuffy.

She glanced at the boys' room. No. At *Sean's* room. She stepped into the doorway, examined the bunk bed against the wall. The covers were pulled back only on the bottom bunk. Sean's bed. The blanket on the top bunk was smooth and unruffled.

No twins. No twins.

Only Sean in this room.

But hadn't she seen him sleeping up there?

Hadn't she brought them both glasses of water? Hadn't she stood in this doorway, arguing with them both about their bedtime?

With a sigh, Jenny spun away. Crossed the hall. Stepped up to the attic door.

She listened for the footsteps overhead.

Silence.

She grabbed the doorknob. Started to turn it.

She screamed as cold, bony fingers wrapped around her hand.

# Chapter 27

*"Jenny — don't!"* A harsh whisper in her ear.

Jenny turned. "Seth — !" she cried. "You're still here!"

His hand felt so clammy against hers.

"Don't let her out," he pleaded. "Please, Jenny — don't let her hurt me again." Seth let go of Jenny's hand. He lowered his head sadly.

"Seth — you — you're real!" Jenny stammered.

She had to make sure. She reached out both hands and grabbed his tiny shoulders. "You're alive!" Jenny declared.

He shook his head. His shoulders trembled beneath her hands. "No, I'm not," he whispered. "I'm not alive."

"Huh?" Jenny jerked back her hands.

"I'm dead, Jenny," Seth murmured, his head still lowered. "I'm dead — because *she* killed me!" He pointed to the attic door.

"But Seth — " Jenny started.

To her surprise, he threw his arms around her waist and held on to her tightly, burying his face in her T-shirt.

She could feel his whole body shaking. She felt hot tears dampen the front of her shirt. "Seth — " she whispered.

"You've been so nice to me," he said in a tiny voice, holding on to her tightly. "I know I was mean to you. But I couldn't help myself. I was so mixed up, Jenny. Because she . . . my baby-sitter . . . she killed me. Killed me for no reason."

A wave of sorrow swept over Jenny. She sifted her hands through his blond hair. So fine and light she could barely feel it.

"Don't let her out, Jenny. She has to stay locked up there. Please don't open the door," Seth pleaded softly, pressing his face against her waist.

"Seth, I don't know — " Jenny started uncertainly. "That girl looks so sad. She — "

"She killed me!" Seth cried. "Jenny — please. You've been so nice. You're the only one who was nice to me. I've lived in this house for so long and — "

"The other kids — " Jenny interrupted.

"Sean and Meredith. They knew you were here. They knew you were a ghost, right, Seth? They talked with you. They played with you."

Seth nodded. "I like them. They were nice to me, too. That's why I made myself look like Sean. I really wanted to be his twin, Jenny. I really wanted to have Sean for a brother."

That's so sad, Jenny thought, feeling tears brim in her eyes. "And they never told their mother about you?" Jenny asked softly.

"They liked me," Seth replied. "They wouldn't tell on me. They kept the secret because they liked me."

"And the howls at night?" Jenny demanded. "The vandalism around the neighborhood? The boy I saw running through my backyard?"

"It was me," Seth confessed, lowering his eyes. "Sometimes I couldn't help myself. Sometimes I had to get out of this house. Sometimes I felt trapped in here. I had to break free."

"You said you were going to kill me," Jenny accused, narrowing her eyes at him, forcing him to look up at her. "You tried to scare me, Seth. You tried to hurt me."

His chest heaved as he let out a sob. "I was so mixed up, Jenny. I didn't really want to hurt you. Sometimes I just couldn't help myself."

Ugly pictures flashed into Jenny's mind. She remembered the cake knife that nearly plunged through her chest. She remembered the roaring garbage disposal, the strong force pushing her hand down into the drain.

She grabbed the door handle.

"No, Jenny!" Seth insisted, his eyes growing wide with fear.

She didn't remove her hand. "Seth, I have to know the truth," she said softly.

"Please." Again, Seth covered her hand with his. "She's bad, Jenny. She's really bad."

"I have to talk to her," Jenny said, clenching her jaw. "I have to see her."

"The door is locked," Seth told her shrilly. "You can't open it. You can't!"

"It's an old door," Jenny replied. "I can pull it open."

"No! *I won't let you!*" he shrieked, his face wild with fear.

Jenny turned the doorknob. And tugged.

The lock gave easily. The door swung open with startling force.

The dark-haired girl burst out, in a long, gray sweater over a black skirt, a triumphant smile on her face.

The smile faded as she gazed at Seth.

And then her eyes glowed red and her mouth twisted in an ugly frown as she turned to Jenny.

"Noooo! Oh no!" Seth screamed. "She killed me, Jenny — and now she's going to kill *you!*"

# Chapter 28

The girl took a lurching step toward Jenny, her pale face twisted in fury. Her dark hair rose up around her head. Her eyes burned like flames.

"Monica — please!" Seth shrieked, backing away. "I warned you, Jenny! I warned you!"

Jenny stumbled back. Hit the wall. "I — I just wanted to help you, Monica," she choked out.

"At last!" the girl cried hoarsely. "At last! At last! After so many years!"

She spun around. Turned her scarlet glare on Seth.

"She killed me, Jenny! She killed me!" Seth cried, his eyes wide with horror.

"Liar!" Monica seethed. "Liar! You killed *me*! You killed *me*, Seth!"

Seth's eyes narrowed. His expression turned hard. He didn't reply.

"You killed me!" Monica repeated, advancing on him. "Locked me in the attic. And then you were so joyful . . . so excited . . . so thrilled by your triumph — you fell down the stairs. You fell and died. What a horrible accident, Seth. A horrible accident took your life — *after* you took mine!"

"Don't listen to her," Seth instructed Jenny. "She'll say anything. We have to lock her back up. We *have* to — before she kills again!"

"For ten years, I've been locked up in that attic," Monica continued, explaining to Jenny. "Unable to rest. Unable to find any peace. Listening to Seth. Listening to him terrify the people who lived in this house."

"Liar!" Seth cried furiously. "People like me. People feel sorry for me — because you killed me. Sean and Meredith *liked* me. They kept my secret because they *liked* me!"

Monica narrowed her dark eyes at Seth. "They kept your secret because you threatened them," she accused. "You hurt them. You said you'd *kill* them if they ever told anyone the truth about you."

Her entire body trembling in fear, Jenny pressed her back against the wall, watching the two ghostly figures rage at each other.

Which one should I believe? Jenny asked herself.

Which one is telling the truth?

She didn't have time to decide.

Monica turned on her, her eyes gleaming red like those of a wild creature. "Thank you for rescuing me, Jenny," she snarled. "I'm really sorry for what I have to do now."

Her eyes glowed even brighter as she advanced on Jenny. Panting excitedly, her hands balled into tight fists, she loomed over Jenny.

"See? I warned you!" Seth called. "I warned you!"

With a soft grunt, Monica grabbed Jenny around the waist — and lifted her easily off the floor.

"Put me down!" Jenny screamed, flailing her arms. "Put me down!"

Ignoring Jenny's terrified pleas, Monica carried her to the stairway.

Lifted her higher.

Jenny thrashed her legs, tried to kick free.

But Monica gripped her with inhuman strength.

She's going to throw me down the stairs! Jenny realized.

"I warned you, Jenny! I warned you!" Seth called from the hallway.

# Chapter 29

Jenny shut her eyes.

Every muscle in her body locked.

She couldn't breathe. She couldn't move.

She waited helplessly for Monica to heave her down, waited for the thud of impact. Waited for the pain to shoot through her body.

To her surprise, Monica set her down gently on her feet.

Jenny's eyes shot open.

Monica had placed her on the top step.

"I want you out of the way," the ghostly girl murmured. "I want you to be safe." She brushed her cheek against Jenny's. "Thank you, Jenny," she whispered. "I'll never forget you."

And, then, before Jenny could react, before Jenny could utter a word, Monica flung herself at Seth.

As Monica tackled him to the floor, Seth

uttered a snarl of rage. Leaning into the hall, Jenny saw his features transform.

The light blond hair appeared to be sucked inside his skull as his head grew and changed shape. His pale skin darkened to a sickening green. Ugly brown sores splotched his bald skull. And he opened his mouth wide to reveal jagged rows of yellow, pointed teeth.

He slashed at Monica with hair-covered claws.

She held on to him tightly, burying her teeth in his neck.

Roaring, biting, thrashing, they wrestled on the floor.

Then, still battling, they were on their feet.

Struggling. Groaning. Howling like wolves. Tangled in each other. Spinning in a furious dance of hatred.

Spinning. Spinning.

Until a whirlwind of black smoke spun around them.

Faster and faster, a dark funnel cloud, swirling around the two ghosts, blanketing them from Jenny's view.

Thick, black smoke, whipping round and around, whistling as it spun, whistling over the angry howls and grunts of pain.

A final hoarse cry.

From Seth? From Monica?

The smoke settled slowly, sinking, sinking into the carpet.

The hallway stood empty.

Empty and silent.

Jenny leaned against the wall, her legs trembling, her heart pounding. She watched the dark smoke lower over the carpet, like a shadow.

And then it was gone.

And the ghosts had vanished with it.

I'm alone now, Jenny thought, letting out a long *whoosh* of air. I'm all alone now.

But, no.

She turned when she heard the voices below her. Voices calling her name.

Lights flashed on downstairs. Mrs. Jeffers peered up the stairs at Jenny. "Huh? You're here?"

Cal appeared beside her mother. He ran up the stairs, put an arm gently around Jenny's shoulder.

"Jenny — what are you *doing* here?" her mother demanded shrilly, her voice revealing her alarm.

"I . . . uh . . . had to see something," Jenny muttered.

"I was so worried," Mrs. Jeffers declared. "I called Cal. I thought maybe you went over there. But . . ."

Cal sniffed the air. "I smell smoke," he said.

"No. It's okay," Jenny assured him. She leaned against him, let him guide her down the steps.

"We searched everywhere," Jenny's mom continued. "Then Cal and I saw a light on over here, and — "

When she reached the bottom of the stairs, Jenny threw her arms around her mother's shoulders and held her close. "I'm okay now, Mom," she told her softly. "Really. I'm okay now. You don't have to worry about me anymore. I've been through a lot. And now I know I'm really strong."

Mrs. Jeffers stared hard at Jenny, as if trying to decide if her words were true. "I — I'm very glad," she finally managed to stammer.

With an arm around each of their waists, Jenny led the way out of the Warsaws' house. The half-moon had found its way out from behind the clouds. The back lawn glistened as if filled with thousands of tiny diamonds.

"You never have to baby-sit again," Mrs. Jeffers told Jenny. "Really. I mean it. No more baby-sitting."

Jenny smiled. "That's okay, Mom," she replied brightly. "I might want to baby-sit again someday. It's a lot more exciting than you think."

Brenda and her friends are planning the perfect
Halloween party . . . and the perfect murder.

**Check out this sneak preview
from R.L. Stine's**

# HALLOWEEN NIGHT

Brenda jumped to her feet, pulling down the
bottom of her black sweatshirt over her faded
jeans. Her friends could see that she was getting worked up. Whenever Brenda got excited,
her face turned bright pink, and the freckles
on her nose and cheeks darkened.

"Halley and I are the same size," Brenda
continued, balling her hands into fists at her
sides. "So she's constantly taking my clothes.
Without asking. And the other night, she
couldn't find her government text. So she took
mine and claimed it was hers."

"Hey, calm down, Brenda," Traci said, sliding to the edge of the bed and lowering her
feet to the floor.

"I can't calm down!" Brenda cried. "She
makes me so mad! I even think she's been flirt-
ing with Ted."

Dina scratched her knee through the black tights. "Are you and Ted going to the Homecoming dance?" she asked, obviously trying to change the subject.

"I guess," Brenda answered, her face still pink, her emerald eyes still flashing with anger.

"Noah and I are going to drop by," Traci said, searching for her sneakers under the bed. "But we're probably not going to stay. School dances are always such a bore."

"Do you have a date?" Brenda asked Dina.

Dina lowered her dark eyes. "Huh-uh," she replied quietly.

"Dina's too tall to date," Traci teased.

"Shut up," Dina snapped.

Traci gaped at her, open-mouthed. "Oh, so now you're so sensitive about being tall, we can't even joke about it?"

"It's not a joke," Dina insisted, staring out the window, her lips drawn in a pout. Suddenly, her expression changed. "Hey, look who's coming!"

"Huh? Who?" Brenda rushed to the window, pushing Dina aside so she could see down to the front yard.

"It's Halley," Dina told Traci. "And guess who she's with? Ted."

"I don't believe this," Brenda muttered.

"Look how she's grinning at him. Isn't that disgusting? I wish a fly would fly into her mouth!"

Traci laughed. Dina continued to stare out the window as Halley and Ted made their way up the driveway. "It's October," she said softly. "All the flies are dead."

"What are they laughing about?" Brenda asked angrily. "What could be so funny?"

"Calm down, Brenda," Traci said, pulling on her left sneaker. "There's no law against walking with Ted, you know."

"There *should* be a law against that disgusting grin!" Brenda declared. "Maybe her face will crack and disintegrate into a thousand pieces."

Traci snickered. "You're cuter than Halley is," she offered, trying to calm her friend down.

"Cute? I don't *want* to be cute!" Brenda cried. "I'm *sick* of being cute!" She pointed down toward the front yard. "Look at her tossing her blonde hair around! That's so cheap!"

Dina glanced at her watch, and her eyes grew wide with horror. "Oh, no! I'm late for work. Dr. Harper will have a fit!"

"Are you still working in that vet's office?" Traci asked, making a face. "Cleaning up after the poodles?"

Dina didn't reply. She jumped up, pushing nervously at the sides of her short brown hair. "Later, guys."

But before she could reach the doorway, Halley walked in. "Hi, everyone!" She grinned at them, pushing her light blonde hair back off her forehead. She wore tight, straight-legged jeans under a magenta V-necked sweater.

Ted entered the room behind her, glancing at Brenda, then quickly looking away.

"How's it going?" Halley asked. Before anyone could reply, she turned to Brenda. "Can I borrow your car? Just for an hour? Ted offered to give me a driving lesson. Isn't that great? You know how nervous I am about the parking exam."

Brenda's mouth dropped open. Her face turned bright pink, and her freckles darkened. "Borrow the car?"

"You don't mind, do you?" Halley asked, smiling at Ted. "We're just going to drive to the mall parking lot so I can practice parking."

"No. Uh . . . okay," Brenda stammered. Biting her lower lip, she made her way to the dresser and picked up the keys to the little blue Geo her dad had bought her for her seventeenth birthday.

She turned back, her eyes on Ted. He had his hands jammed into his jeans pockets. His mop of curly brown hair was unbrushed, as usual.

Brenda handed the keys to Halley. "Call me later," she told Ted. "After dinner. Maybe we can study the math together."

"Yeah. Good. See you later." He turned and made his way quickly out of the room.

Halley closed her hand around the car keys. "See you. I'll try not to total it," she said. She hurried after Ted.

Brenda listened to their footsteps going down the stairs. Then she turned to her two friends. "Do you believe it?" she cried. "She takes my boyfriend and my car, and doesn't even say thanks or anything? Do you *believe* it?"

"I have an idea," Traci said, her silvery eyes lighting up with excitement. She stepped up beside Brenda.

"What kind of idea?" Brenda asked skeptically.

"Let's murder her!" Traci suggested.

## About the Author

R. L. STINE is the author of the series *Fear Street*, *Nightmare Room*, *Give Yourself Goosebumps*, and the phenomenally successful *Goosebumps*. His thrilling teen titles have sold more than 250 million copies internationally — enough to earn him a spot in the *Guinness Book of World Records*! Mr. Stine lives in New York City with his wife, Jane, and his son, Matt.